D0556848

COCHRANE

5 - JUN 2018

A Wedding
and a
White Christmas

ЗИАЯНЭОЭ

Also by Suzanne Stengl

The Ghost and Christie McFee

Angel Wings

The Thurston Heirloom

~ Series ~

Something Old
Something New

A Wedding and a White Christmas

On the Way to a Wedding

Wedding Bell Blues (coming soon)

A Wedding
and a
White Christmas

Something Old, Something New
Book 1

Suzanne Stengl

Copyright 2017 Suzanne Stengl
All rights reserved.

ISBN 978-1-7751464-0-7

This is a work of fiction. All of the characters, organizations, and events
portrayed in this novel are either products of the author's imagination
or are used fictitiously.

This book or any portion of it may not be reproduced or used in any
manner whatsoever without the express written permission of the
publisher except for the use of brief quotations in a book review.

Publisher: Mya & Angus
Cover Design: Tammy Seidick

www.suzannestengl.com

MYA & ANGUS

To Rolf,

for everything

Chapter One

What happens in Vegas . . .

With her life officially at rock bottom, Emily Farrell sat in the seventh row of the Boeing 737 by the window on the starboard side.

Mark Bainbridge sat next to her in the middle seat. "Don't look so worried," he said.

Mark was three years older than Emily, had been her next-door neighbor when they were growing up and—until last night—he'd been her best friend in the whole world. Right now, she didn't know what he was.

Following them in to the cabin, Emily's friend Catherine banged her carry-on against the aisle seat, and then stepped into the row to get out of the way of other boarding passengers. "That was crazy last night," she said, as she dropped her purse and coat on the seat. She lifted her carry-on and slid it into the overhead compartment, then stuffed her coat up there too.

Soon they would be back to the cold December weather in Calgary. Emily leaned close to Mark. "We're not telling anyone about this, right?"

"Probably we should keep it to ourselves," he said. "Your aunt would have a heart attack if she knew."

"Your Aunt Myra?" Catherine piped up. "If she knew what?"

"If she knew how much alcohol was involved last

night," Mark said without missing a beat.

"What happens in Vegas, stays in Vegas." Catherine closed the overhead compartment and scanned the back of the plane. "Besides, it was her idea for us to do the Jack and Jill celebration here."

Although Las Vegas specialized in pre-wedding parties, Emily hadn't thought much of the idea. She'd only come for her sister. And, oddly enough, Mark had wanted to come too. He was the sensible influence in the group, normally, so it had seemed like a good idea at the time.

"Your aunt wanted everyone to do their partying way ahead of your sister's wedding," Catherine said. And then, as if she could not resist, she added, "It would be awful to have a repeat performance of last summer."

Emily closed her eyes, remembered that warm summer night last June. Catherine didn't know what had happened because Emily had not talked about it. Not to anyone.

"Sorry, Emily, but you blew it." Catherine paused, as if she were letting her comment sink in. "Oh well, you and Dan will get back together some day. I'm sure of it." She was standing, looking at the rear of the plane. "What did you guys do last night?"

"Cruised the strip," Mark said, with a lighthearted tone. "You?"

"Took in the show at Caesars, and then ended up at the blackjack table at Bellagio. Dan broke even. I thought he'd do better than that. He told me he could count cards."

"Dan tends to exaggerate," Emily said.

Catherine ignored her. "Have you seen your sister? Never mind, there she is. I'll be back in a minute." And then Catherine was gone, squeezing past a long line of bunched-up passengers struggling with their luggage.

An awkward silence filled the small space between Emily and Mark. She stared at the shiny edge of the onboard magazine in the seat pocket in front of her.

Behind the magazine was the safety card and an airsickness bag. She pulled out the safety card, flipped it open and scanned for escape routes.

Finally, as the silence went on, she closed the card and, without making eye contact, leaned over to Mark again. "Are you going to tell Judith?"

"That's not really serious."

It never was serious with Mark. "But are you going to tell her?"

"Better not. Anyway, nothing happened."

His voice was light, cheerful even. How could he be so calm?

She turned to look at him.

He relaxed in his seat, his head back, eyes straight ahead. The picture of composure. His dark tousled hair brushed his collar. With the rush for the airport, he hadn't shaved this morning so beard stubble shadowed his jaw. Regardless, he looked easygoing and friendly. And although he hadn't had much time for sleep last night, he looked rested.

Another moment passed. Whether he liked it or not, they had to talk about it. She took a deep breath and made herself say the words. "Are we really married?"

The corner of his mouth quirked, as if he might laugh. "Unfortunately, yes." A short pause, and then, "I didn't exactly mean unfortunately, but—"

"I know what you mean." She sighed, and still couldn't quite believe it. Last night, after way too much wine, she and Mark had been married by an Elvis impersonator.

Mark shrugged. "It's not like it was consummated," he said.

No, it wasn't, but . . . "We did kiss."

"Did we? I can't remember."

Emily remembered. For all the years she'd known Mark, she'd never kissed him, and she'd had no idea he could kiss like that.

"Not consummated," he repeated, "so it will probably be easy to deal with. Probably just a quick annulment. I'll talk to Pro tomorrow."

Please let it be quick, Emily thought. Aunt Myra would be so upset if she found out.

"No one needs to know," he said. He turned his head to look at her, the warm deep brown of his eyes reflecting genuine affection. "We'll deal with the paperwork and then it will be over." He reached for her hand and squeezed.

The familiar reassuring touch had its effect and she felt her shoulders slump.

"It will be a funny story someday," he said. "Don't worry. I'll take care of it."

The flight attendant appeared and glanced at her chart. "Mark and Emily?"

Mark looked up. "Yes?"

"So you're the happy couple. The chapel has sent champagne. I'll bring it once we're at altitude."

Emily felt her chest tighten. The last thing she needed was for Catherine to find out what she and Mark had so stupidly done. Catherine would tell everyone. "Uh, no," Emily said. "Thank you very much but . . . we don't drink."

And then Mark added, "You can pass the champagne on to another couple. Surprise them."

"I understand," the flight attendant said.

Yes, she probably did. She'd probably seen many similar scenarios on the Las Vegas to Calgary flight.

"Oh," Mark said, as if he'd had a sudden thought. "One more thing. We're keeping it under wraps until we tell our parents." He sent the flight attendant his trademark thousand kilowatt smile.

"Of course." She smiled back and checked her list again. "Also, the chapel sent a package. Do you have an address you'd like it delivered to?"

Mark took her clipboard, wrote out his address and

handed it back. The flight attendant disappeared.

A second later, Catherine returned. "Noelle and Troy are at the very back. They said they really liked their Jack and Jill Party," she reported. "Even though we all got separated."

Mark laughed. "That's probably why they liked it so much."

"They went on one of those helicopter rides over the city. And then Troy said they checked out an Elvis Chapel. Can you believe it? He wanted to get married right away."

In the background, the flight attendant had started the pre-flight demo.

> *In the unlikely event of a change in cabin pressure, the panels above your seat will open revealing oxygen masks.*

Emily wished she had an oxygen mask right now, already feeling short of breath, especially with Catherine on a roll, again.

"That would not have gone over well with your aunt," Catherine said, her voice drowning out the safety instructions. "After all the work she's done for Noelle's Christmas Eve wedding, that would simply break her heart. Especially after Emily's wedding."

"Emily's almost wedding." Mark corrected her.

"Botched wedding, you mean. I still can't believe she walked out on Dan. The two of them are perfect for each other."

Emily leaned in front of Mark, waved to get Catherine's attention. Keeping her tone hushed, she said, "Can we please talk about something else?"

"Emily was ready to get married," Catherine told Mark, apparently unwilling to talk about something else. "And then she got a bad case of cold feet."

"I'm sitting right here, you know. While you discuss my life."

"Don't be so sensitive."

Emily drew back and slouched in her seat. She wished the throbbing in her head would stop. And she wished that Catherine would stop—or at least lower her voice. "Advil," Emily said. "I need Advil."

"And lots of fluids," Catherine advised. "I'll flag down an attendant as soon as this useless presentation is over. Does anybody ever listen to this stuff?"

> *Breathe normally. The plastic bag will not fully inflate, although oxygen is flowing. Secure your own mask before helping others.*

Emily tried to listen to the flight attendant, and tried to block out Catherine as she continued talking to Mark about last June's failed wedding, making no attempt to keep her voice down.

It had failed at the rehearsal dinner, the night before what would have been the wedding. The night before the summer solstice.

Aunt Myra had thought a Summer Solstice wedding would be beautiful for Emily. She also thought a Christmas Eve wedding would be beautiful for Noelle. And their aunt was determined to stage at least one wedding this year.

She wanted it to be at her Country Club, but Noelle had refused. Noelle and Troy would make their vows at home, in front of the fireplace.

> *Please take a moment to locate your nearest two exits, keeping in mind that the closest exits may be behind you.*

Instinctively Emily glanced around for the exits, found them and memorized them. She tugged her seat belt, making it extra tight.

"Are you listening?" Catherine asked.

"To what?"

"To me! I said we need to plan Noelle's bridal shower. That's supposed to be your job. You're the maid of honor. You can't put it off any longer. The wedding is in less than three weeks." After a breath, she added, "My wedding is going to be a lot more organized than this."

"Noelle doesn't want a shower."

"Of course she does. Now we need a theme."

Catherine might need a theme, but Emily needed some quiet.

"Don't you just buy toasters or something?" Mark asked.

"Shut up, Mark." Catherine leaned forward, looking across Mark to see Emily. "Maybe we'll do china." A short pause, and then, "She does have a pattern picked out, doesn't she?"

"I don't know. I don't think so. She doesn't care about china patterns."

"What?" Catherine grimaced.

"I said she doesn't care about—"

"Never mind," Catherine said. "I'll pick out a pattern."

Emily gripped the armrests and sucked in another deep breath. "My head hurts."

Catherine huffed and pressed the overhead call button.

"What are you doing?" Mark reached up and canceled the light.

"Getting her some Advil. They must have Advil on board."

"Not now. We're ready to takeoff."

"So? How hard can it be to—"

"She'll be all right," Mark said. "Let her close her eyes until we're in the air."

"Oh. I forgot. Emily's afraid of flying." A quick sigh. "But then, she's afraid of everything." Catherine retrieved her purse from under the seat and found her cell phone.

"Put your purse back," Emily told her. "Are you even supposed to have your cell phone out?"

"It's in flight mode. I'm making a list." Catherine shoved her purse under the seat in front of her, and then she busied herself with her list making.

"Lean on the headrest," Mark said. He reached for Emily's hand again. "I'll hold your hand during takeoff."

He tilted his head toward her and, in a low voice that Catherine could not hear, he said, "Are you ever going to tell me what happened that night?"

"I don't want to talk about it."

"I know," he said. "But someday you'll tell me."

By now, the aircraft had finished taxiing into position on the runway. Emily felt the rumble of the engines, the banked power vibrating up through her feet as they picked up speed, approaching the point of no return. And then with a sudden flutter, the plane left the ground and they were in the air.

Chapter Two

The elevator dinged at the twenty-seventh floor of the Sun Valley Tower and Dr. Mark Bainbridge reluctantly stepped out. In front of him, the glass doors of Jones Jamieson, Barristers & Solicitors, sparkled in the sunlight from the windows beyond.

Having to meet Pro like this was embarrassing, and Mark wanted to turn around and head back out into the chilly December Monday.

Mark and Pro had made fun of their friend Ryder, getting engaged last month, to Catherine of all people. And their friend Logan was in a serious relationship. At least, Logan's girlfriend thought so.

Pro had met both women and was not particularly impressed. In an attempt to be helpful, he was advising prenup agreements.

Standing in front of the glass doors, Mark pressed his palms against his forehead. He could hardly believe what he'd done.

After all their kidding around about not settling down, it turned out he was the first one of their group to get married. Him. The guy who'd never had a serious relationship in his life.

No matter. It wasn't a real marriage. It wasn't something he or Emily wanted. It was simple paperwork that needed to be taken care of, privately, so Emily would not have to suffer any embarrassment. Any *more* embarrassment. She'd had enough of that last summer.

He could have called Pro, could have asked him to meet for a beer, and could have discussed the situation casually. But he wanted expert advice and he was going to pay his friend for it.

Straightening his shoulders, he pushed through the doors and approached the reception desk. "Mark Bainbridge for Prometheus Jones."

"I'll let him know you're here." The receptionist smiled, tilting her head in a cutesy way that said she was interested. In him.

Any other time, he would have flirted with her. He enjoyed flirting, enjoyed the game. The lightness, the pleasure without commitment.

But not today.

He took a seat so he could face the view of the snow-covered mountains to the west. It had finally stopped snowing about an hour ago. Road crews busied themselves clearing the main roads and traffic inched along.

When they'd returned from Las Vegas yesterday, the full force of winter had slammed into them. Blizzard conditions delayed their landing and Emily had been terrified as they'd circled the airport for a half hour.

Finally the storm let up enough to allow a safe landing and he'd practically had to pry her fingers from the armrests. He'd offered to drive her to her apartment but she wanted to be alone. So he'd bundled her into a taxi and promised her he'd deal with their . . . *problem* . . . first thing in the morning.

So here he was, keeping his promise.

He glanced at the coffee table in front of him . . . the pile of magazines, new ones with crisp edges, all arranged in neat cascading stacks so the titles could be seen.

In the center of the table was a Christmas ornament. He supposed it was a Christmas tree. The base was a six inch round of wood, probably cedar, because it smelled like freshly cut cedar. A hole had been drilled in the middle of the base and a thin pine branch extended from it. A shiny red ball hung from the branch and a strand of silver beads twirled around it. It looked childish and elegant at the same time. And hopeful, like a promise of Christmas.

"His aunt made it," the receptionist said.

"His Aunt Tizzy?" Of course, his aunt would have made it.

"Have you met her?" The pretty receptionist smiled, an obvious attempt to engage him.

"Yes, I have," Mark said. "She's . . ."

"She's quite a character," the receptionist supplied. Then the switchboard rang, and she answered.

Mark picked up a magazine and pretended to read it. In all the years he'd known Pro, he'd never been to the guy's office. They'd all been friends in high school. Pro, Ryder, Logan and Mark. They'd graduated the same year at Aberton, and then they'd all gone on to U of C. Logan and Ryder in engineering, Pro in law, and Mark in medicine.

Now Logan had a petroleum exploration company—in this building, one floor down. Ryder owned a construction company. Pro had his law firm and Mark was in his final year of residency in orthopedics at the Nose Hill Hospital.

"Mark?" Pro said, coming out to the reception area to meet him.

"Hi." Mark dropped the magazine, stood and they shook hands. It seemed odd, meeting like this. They only ever met on weekends, skiing in the winter, hiking in the summer. Sometimes they played squash at the university courts. Sometimes they met with the old group to toss a football in the park.

"I'm back here," Pro said as he led the way. He wore

his lawyer uniform of navy pinstripe suit with a dark blue shirt and gold silk tie.

Mark didn't even own a suit. Today he wore jeans and a polo shirt but his working uniform was the hospital issue green scrubs.

They entered a large corner office with a bank of windows straight ahead and another bank of windows to the right. Floor-to-ceiling windows. Pro's desk was on the left side of the room.

Behind the desk was a large painting of a tropical landscape, a terrace with white tables and flower-laced arbors—red flowers—probably meant to be bougainvillea. Clay pots of the bougainvillea cascaded from the terrace to white stone steps leading to a greenish blue sea. In the distance, sail boats glided in front of rocky white cliffs.

"Nice painting," Mark said.

"Thanks. Have a seat." Pro sank into his desk chair and picked up a file folder.

In the corner beside the desk, a fig tree reached its leafy branches toward the light and one branch brushed against the window. Little red balls decorated the lower branches, along with two other ornaments—tiny red cardinals, placed side by side as if they were having a conversation.

An oak credenza stood in front of the windowed wall across from Pro's desk and displayed a dozen, or more, miniature airplane replicas, and a little figurine of a bean with writing on it.

Mark picked it up and read the words out loud. "Lawyers are appealing human beans?"

"Aunt Tizzy," Pro said as if it explained everything. And it did. He opened the file and started to read. "What's up? My assistant said this is about . . . an annulment?" He frowned, searching the file for an explanation. "Did you get married somewhere along the line?"

Mark inhaled, then let out a long sigh. He took a seat in front of the desk. "You know Emily's little sister is getting married?"

"Of course I do," Pro said. "I'm invited to the wedding." He shuffled through some papers in the folder and tapped them together. "They had the stag party this past weekend. In Las Vegas," he added. "I was invited but I had to cancel at the last minute."

"Yes. Stag. Stagette," Mark said. "They call it a Jack and Jill party."

"All right." Pro watched him, waiting. "A Jack and Jill party."

"I was there," Mark said. He tapped his fingers on the edge of the desk.

Pro leaned back in his chair. "Go on."

Mark coughed, and cleared his throat. "Emily and I got married. In one of those Elvis chapels."

Pro's mouth dropped open, he stared, and then he started to laugh.

"It's not funny."

"I think it's funny." Pro shrugged his shoulders back and looked serious, but only for a second, and then laughed some more.

Mark got up, crossed to the credenza, picked up an airplane replica, and studied it.

After a few moments, Pro transformed back to his business self. "So what do you need my help with?"

"An annulment."

"Okaaay." A short pause. "Have you thought about this?"

"What is there to think about?"

"You and Emily. You're always together. You make a great couple."

They weren't always together, not anymore. Not since Dan had proposed, and that was almost a year ago. But they were still friends. "We're friends and we'd like to keep it that way."

Pro put his hands on the chair arms and straightened. "If you're in love, it's not like marriage and friendship are mutually exclusive."

"Marriage usually happens when two people are in love, not just friends. Besides there's all that prenup stuff you're always talking about. We didn't do any of that," Mark said, pacing the room.

"You want a prenup?" Pro rubbed his palms together. "I can work with that."

"I don't want a prenup. It's a little late for that. I want an annulment." Mark walked back to his chair and collapsed into it. "Anyway, it's a rebound thing. For her."

Pro fell silent. After a moment, he said, "You mean the Dan thing last summer."

"Yeah, that."

Mark remembered that night all too clearly. He'd left the reception to go outside and see where Emily had gone. And then he saw her running up the path from the pond, crossing under the arbor. She'd seen him, grabbed hold of his hands, and asked him to drive her home. At the time, home was her Aunt Myra's.

It was a long drive, and she hadn't said a word, not one word. Her pretty blonde hair had come loose from its elaborate style and the gold strands wisped around her shoulders. Her blue eyes had shimmered with unshed tears, making her look so fragile. But she hadn't cried, and she hadn't talked. That in itself was amazing.

And, he hadn't tried to get her to talk. It had barely happened. She wasn't ready. When he'd pulled into the driveway, she'd rushed out of the car and run inside.

"This is all confidential," Mark said. "I don't want anyone finding out we're married."

"Of course, it's all confidential." Pro looked somewhat

affronted. And then, "Does Judith know?"

"Seriously?"

"Are you going to tell her?"

"No."

Pro thought about that and then he pushed the file away and reclined back in his chair. "I never saw Emily and Dan as a good match."

Mark squinted at his friend. "You're a lawyer, Pro, not a matchmaker. Now how do we get an annulment?"

"You mean a divorce."

"No, I mean an annulment. It wasn't . . . consummated."

Pro blinked, a few seconds passed, and then he said, "*Emily* wants the marriage ended?"

"Of course she does. She wants it yesterday."

"Okay." Pro shifted into lawyer mode. "First of all, you need a divorce."

"But—"

"Consummation does not legalize a marriage as far as the law is concerned, nor is the lack of sex considered valid grounds for an annulment."

"But—"

"Neither of you is physically incapable of sexual relations or impotent?"

"Uh . . . no."

"Then legally, a divorce would apply here, not an annulment."

Mark stared at his friend. "Really?"

"It's a common misconception," Pro said. "People think it's easier to get an annulment, but it's not. An annulment is more costly and difficult."

"Okay," Mark said, nodding. "So, now what?"

"To get an uncontested divorce in Alberta, you need to live apart for one year."

"A year?" Not what he'd expected, not at all. "A whole year?"

"It's a good thing," Pro said. "Neither of you can remarry during that time."

"So . . ."

"So, even if she patches things up with Dan, she can't marry him until this divorce goes through."

Mark felt a sudden ray of lightness fill his mind. Maybe a year was a good thing. "She can't marry Dan," he said, thinking about it. "Not until this divorce goes through?"

"That is correct."

"And it will take a year?"

"You need to live apart for a year," Pro repeated. "You're not living together now are you?"

"No. We've never lived together."

"You've been next-door neighbors since . . ."

"Since a long time. But not anymore. Neither of us lives with family now."

"I know *you* don't. When did Emily move out?"

"Right after the rehearsal dinner." Mark had helped her to move.

"I thought she was out of a job?"

"She is. But she's got a part-time job working in a library, re-shelving books or something. And she has some savings."

"I'm surprised her aunt let her move out."

"Her aunt wasn't home that weekend."

They both knew Myra Wright. She'd become the guardian for Emily and Noelle when they were young girls and she'd pretty much decided their destiny from that point on.

Well, not at first, according to what Mark's father remembered.

Apparently, the young girls had been a handful for their maiden aunt. But then Myra had been hospitalized with pneumonia for a month. After that, it seemed like Emily and Noelle tiptoed around the woman, afraid they might end up back in foster care. Even all these years later, they still deferred to Myra, way too much.

"She didn't want to live with her aunt anymore, not after . . . not after the wedding was canceled."

"All right." Pro picked up his pen and a yellow pad of paper. "You live apart for a year."

"Easy. Then what?"

"After that it will take about three months for the paperwork to go through."

"Another three months. Good." Well, not exactly good, but it didn't matter, did it? He was in no hurry to get married. And judging by the way Emily had impulsively married him, it was better if she couldn't rush into anything else.

Pro was staring at him.

"What?"

Pro scanned the file again and cleared his throat. "In the meantime, get me a copy of the marriage certificate from Las Vegas."

"Where do I get it from?"

"The Clark County Recorder's Office. You can find them online."

"I'll do it right away."

"No rush," Pro said, as he wrote on the yellow pad. "When did you get married?"

"Saturday night." Or maybe it was early Sunday morning. He wasn't sure.

"The marriage certificate may not be there yet."

"Why not?"

"Whoever performs the ceremony has ten days to submit the documentation." Pro turned his computer screen so Mark could see it. "You got married on Saturday, so wait ten days. Wait until the fifteenth. By then the marriage will be recorded and you can order a certified marriage certificate."

"Can I do it online?"

"Most people do."

"The Clark County Recorder's Office?"

"Right. And it will take about three weeks for it to be mailed."

Mark turned on his phone, scrolled to his calendar, and made a note. "I'll contact them on the fifteenth."

Pro wrote something else on the file, and then closed it. He leaned back in his chair.

"Did Ryder go to Vegas?"

"No. He had to work."

"And Catherine was okay with that?"

"She didn't say anything." But, Mark knew, Catherine was not happy with Ryder's decision. Catherine was never happy if things didn't go her way. She was even unhappy about Emily breaking things off with Dan, and that was none of Catherine's business.

"Did Dan go to Vegas?" Pro asked.

"Yes," Mark answered. "Catherine invited him."

"How did that work?"

"We avoided him."

"I see."

And it had been satisfying, avoiding the idiot. And not only that, it had been like old times, being with Emily.

Pro turned to his computer, tapped a few keys, waited, and leaned back again. "Are you at the hospital today?" he asked.

"I'm heading over there now. Why?"

"Can you check on anyone in orthopedics?"

"Of course. I'm the chief resident."

"Good," Pro said. "My aunt was admitted last Friday. That's why I couldn't go the stag. I mean, the Jack and Jill party."

That didn't sound good. "Your Aunt Tizzy? What happened?"

"She was up on a ladder, stringing lights on her tree, and she slipped."

Mark had a flash of anxiety, then shook it off and went into doctor mode. "How is she?"

"I don't think she broke anything, but they're keeping her for observation. She's not pleased. Says she's got too much to do to be sitting around in a hospital." Pro looked at the desk, his brow creased with worry. "You know what she's like."

Mark knew. Aunt Tizzy was Pro's only relative, had raised him like a son, and was the kindest aunt anyone could ask for. Even if she was a touch eccentric.

"I'll look in on her and give you a call."

"Thanks. I appreciate it."

Chapter Three

When the snow lay round about, deep and crisp and even

Catherine Forsythe rang the bell, opened the door, and poked her head inside. A strand of Christmas bells on the doorknob made little tinkling sounds. "Myra?"

"Come on in!" Myra's voice called from the kitchen.

Catherine stepped out of the cold and into the warmth of Myra Wright's estate home. The smells of warm cinnamon and pine needles filled the air, the pine coming from the huge Christmas tree straight ahead of her on the other side of the stair railing.

From the entrance, a hall led to the back of the house, where Myra was, and a flight of stairs descended to the basement. A spindled railing ran between the stairs on the left and the hall on the right.

The stairs were open to the top floor, making it possible to see into the living room from the entrance, and making it possible to display the Christmas tree to the best advantage.

That was one of the things Catherine appreciated about her friend Myra. The woman knew how to decorate. They'd met a year ago when Catherine had joined Myra's book club. And they discovered they shared many of the same tastes in books, furnishings and theater. Even though Myra was much older than Catherine, the two had become good friends.

Catherine got out of her boots, lined them up on the mat by the door, and wondered if Noelle was home today or already back at work.

She might be downstairs, either in the rec room or her suite. Up until last summer, Emily had lived down there too, in the suite opposite Noelle's. The rec room had a fireplace and a walkout to the backyard and patio. It was a perfectly comfortable place to live and yet, for some reason, Emily had decided to move out. Silly girl.

To the right of the entrance and behind a set of French doors, rolls of Christmas wrapping paper took up all the space on the desk in Myra's office.

Catherine stuffed her mitts in her coat pocket, hung her coat in the closet to the left of the entrance and turned to gaze at the Christmas tree again. Then she followed the hall to the kitchen and the smell of cinnamon.

"Have a seat," Myra instructed as she clattered a pan out of the oven and up onto the stove top. A tray of cinnamon buns. One of Myra's specialties.

Four barstools lined up at the shiny granite counter that divided the kitchen from the dining room. Catherine sat on a stool, leaned her back against the counter and looked out at the view.

Sighing, she wondered how best to break the news. Myra would not be happy when she heard. Not after all her careful planning.

The bay window in the dining room presented a backyard of Christmas-card-perfect evergreens, their boughs weighted with heaps of brilliant white snow.

On the patio, the ring of cinder blocks around the fire pit lay hidden under snow drifts. It had finally stopped snowing but ice crystals still sparkled in the air and twinkled on the snow, and the cold temperatures remained. What a contrast from Las Vegas yesterday.

"Tea?"

"Please."

"I know you like it with milk, but this tastes best with lemon."

Please, not lemon. Catherine didn't like lemon, but there was no use arguing. And of course, arguing took effort and she felt so frustrated she could not handle one more argument. Besides, it was only tea. She looked at the living room and the tree.

An open concept design connected the living room on the left, then the fireplace, then the dining room. The living room and dining room both had bay windows showcasing the beautiful backyard.

In the living room, the perfectly proportioned Christmas tree looked like something out of a magazine. Little white lights glowed, reflecting off gold balls and garlands of twisted gold ribbon. Instead of a star, a satin angel topped the tree. Catherine would have preferred a star, but Myra liked angels.

The clink of china, and then the sound of pouring liquid went on behind her. She took a long breath. How was she going to say it. She couldn't just blurt it out.

Fire flickered in the gas fireplace in the living room. Flames danced along the ceramic logs looking cheery on this winter day. She had a vague thought that a real fireplace, a wood-burning one, would be nicer. But a gas fireplace was more efficient and gave out a fair amount of heat. And besides, who wanted to deal with the mess of sweeping up ashes?

"Well?" Myra asked. "Aren't you going to tell me about Las Vegas?"

Catherine turned around and watched Myra finish preparing tea at the counter beside the stove. Might as well get it over with. "It didn't work," Catherine mumbled.

"What do you mean, it didn't work?" Myra wrinkled her forehead, as if she hadn't heard right, and then set a steaming cup of tea on the counter in front of Catherine.

The cup was Myra's Christmas china, with a pattern of holly sprigs. The woman seemed to have china for every occasion. Catherine sipped the tea—a blend that tasted like oranges and cloves. And lemon, too.

"I mean it didn't work," Catherine said. "They didn't spend any time together."

Back at the counter, Myra used a purple plastic spatula to lift a gooey cinnamon bun out of the aluminum tray. She arranged the bun on a matching china tea plate, added a fork, and then brought the plate to the counter.

"They must have spent some time together," she said. "They were on the same plane, for heaven's sake."

Knowing Myra wanted a full report on the Jack and Jill party, Catherine carefully arranged her china cup on its saucer. "Nothing happened."

"They didn't patch things up?" Myra folded her hands and pressed them against her heart.

"They didn't talk. They didn't meet."

"You mean she didn't spend *any* time with Dan?"

"No," Catherine said. "She didn't."

"No time at all?" Myra still held her hands in a prayer position, as if that might make a difference.

"Not one minute." And it wasn't like Catherine hadn't done her best to engineer a meeting. "Mark spoiled everything. He shouldn't have come."

With a quick swoosh and a humph, Emily's aunt threw her hands to her sides. "Mark." She said his name as if it explained everything. A moment later, she spun around and marched back to the cupboard next to the stove. There was a rattle of china as Myra retrieved a teacup, and then she slammed the cupboard door.

At least she hadn't slammed the cup. Catherine took another sip of tea and couldn't help crinkling her nose.

"Mark is the last person Emily needs to be with. That

boy doesn't understand the first thing about commitment. He's a horrible influence." Myra poured her tea and raged on. "When he was growing up, he was constantly switching girlfriends." She picked up a wedge of lemon and crushed it—mangled it—as she squeezed it into the hot liquid. "Never stayed with anyone. I'd barely get introduced to one girl and he was going out with another." She paused, staring at her tea. "This is so awful."

For a second, Catherine thought Myra meant the tea was awful. Obviously, she meant the situation with Emily and Dan. And, of course, that was awful, and frustrating. Myra only wanted what was best for her nieces and Emily should have made up with Dan by now.

Catherine traced her finger along the rim of the cup, recalling that summer night last June. The fairy lights were strung on the trees outside the Country Club, and she saw Emily running from under the arbor in the garden. A moment later, Dan came chasing after her.

Something had gone terribly wrong and there was nothing Catherine could say to Emily to find out what it was. And now, almost six months later, it still seemed like the relationship was doomed. "Maybe they're not meant to be a couple."

"Don't be ridiculous. Of course they are." Myra took a stack of poinsettia-patterned serviettes from the cupboard and plunked them on the counter. Then she got herself a saucer. "Who invited him anyway?"

"If you mean Mark, Noelle invited him."

"Noelle? Why would she invite Mark? He'd only get in the way. And the whole point of the Jack and Jill party was to get Emily and Dan back together."

Catherine closed her eyes, and then chose her best diplomatic tone. "The whole point of the Jack and Jill Party was to celebrate Noelle and Troy's upcoming wedding."

"I know. I know," Myra said. "But this would have been perfect."

Footsteps sounded on the stairs from the basement rec room. Maybe Noelle *was* home? And if she was, had she heard them talking? Catherine did a quick search through her last bits of conversation.

"What would have been perfect?" Noelle came down the hall with her carryall looped over her shoulder. It was the same poinsettia bag she'd had on the plane yesterday— a large bag with a beige canvas front and back, green fabric sides with a leafy pattern, and a green handle of the same material. A bright red fabric poinsettia decorated the front canvas panel. Definitely in the Christmas spirit. Probably purchased in Las Vegas.

"Hi, Catherine."

"Hi, Noelle." Deciding nothing terrible had been overheard, Catherine clutched her fork and tasted the cinnamon bun. The warm spiciness melted in her mouth. Myra could be interfering but she was an excellent cook.

After hanging her bag on the back of a dining room chair, Noelle made a beeline for the kitchen counter. "Aunt Myra? What would have been perfect?" Noelle asked again. She was at the counter, using the purple spatula to dig out a bun.

"The cinnamon buns, dear. I don't think I used enough butter."

Good recovery, Catherine thought, knowing how Noelle hated it when her Aunt Myra tried to meddle.

The Christmas bells on the front door knob jingled, and a blast of frigid air blew into the house. Noelle set her bun on a plate, dashed around the counter and stepped into the hall. "Hi, Frank! You're just in time for cinnamon buns!" Without any more of a welcome, she came back to the counter and busied herself with getting some extra bits of raisins out of the pan and onto her plate.

Frank Bainbridge was Myra's next-door neighbor. He was also Mark's father.

"I shoveled your walk," the old man called from the entrance.

Myra leaned across the bar to speak to Catherine. "Does he have his dog with him?" she asked in a hushed voice.

Catherine craned her head to look down the hall and saw the Labradoodle sitting on the mat, contently lapping the ice out of her paws. Frank had looped her leash on the door handle.

"You're not going to leave her there?" Catherine called.

"She's defrosting," Frank said, as he removed his boots. A minute later, he entered the kitchen. Without being invited, he opened the cupboards next to the stove, got himself a mug and poured himself some tea. Then he helped himself to a cinnamon bun, pinching it out of the tray with his fingers. "I hate this floor," he said.

"What's wrong with the floor?" Catherine asked.

"Myra had to put in tile."

"I like tile." Myra bristled. "It's easy to clean."

"It's cold on my feet."

Catherine closed her eyes and inhaled, slowly. How these two old people tolerated each other was a mystery.

Myra leveled a glance at Frank. "Your son got in the way. He spoiled everything."

Frank bit into the cinnamon bun, smiled as he tasted it, and then looked at Myra. "What?" he asked, talking around a mouthful.

"Mark went to the Jack and Jill party in Las Vegas."

Frank kept eating. "What's a Jack and Jill party?"

"It's a pre-wedding party," Catherine said.

Frank shrugged. "I suppose one more party can't hurt."

"Don't you understand?" Myra's lips flattened to a thin straight line.

"All I understand is this floor is damn cold."

"Then bring your slippers when you visit."

"Every time I visit? I'm supposed to bring my slippers?"

"Frank," Catherine intervened. "Buy an extra pair and leave them by the door."

"I'm not buying an extra pair of slippers."

"Oh, for heaven's sake," Myra said. "I'll buy you some slippers for Christmas."

Quietly avoiding the commotion, Noelle had slipped onto the barstool at the end of the counter.

"Never mind," Myra said, huffing out a sigh. "I should have made sure you knew. You could have kept him home."

"Kept him home? In case you haven't noticed, he doesn't live with me. And if his friends were going to Las Vegas, why shouldn't he go?"

Giving up on Frank, Myra turned around and zeroed in on Noelle.

"Has Emily decided when to host the bridal shower?"

"I don't want a bridal shower," Noelle said, licking sticky cinnamon off her fingers. "We haven't even returned Emily's shower and wedding gifts."

"We're not returning them. She's still getting married. She has a few issues to work out. That's all."

"Right," Noelle said. "A few issues."

Frank went to the fridge and retrieved a jug of milk.

"What are you doing?"

"I like milk in my tea."

"You don't put milk in that tea. You add lemon."

"I don't like lemon," Frank said, as he added a dollop of milk to his tea. "I like milk."

Myra glanced up at the ceiling, seemed to count, and then refocused on Noelle. "You weren't much help."

"Me?" Noelle dabbed her fingers on a serviette. "Much help with what?"

"With the Jack and Jill party." Pressing her hands onto the granite top of the counter, Myra looked like she was trying to hold on to her damaged plans. "You could have done something to make sure your sister and Dan spent time together."

Noelle's mouth dropped open. "It was *my* Jack and Jill. I'm not responsible for getting Emily back together with her ex."

"Kid's got a point," Frank said, reaching for a second cinnamon bun.

Myra slapped his hand, got a plate and arranged the bun on it. Then she handed it to him, along with a fork and one of the poinsettia-patterned napkins.

"We need to think of some other way." Myra paced between the fridge and the counter. "Are you sure you can't have Dan in the wedding party?"

"Aunt Myra. I'll just pretend you didn't say that."

"But—"

"No buts. Troy hardly knows Dan."

"I'll talk to Troy myself," Myra said to nobody in particular.

"Don't do that. He's already thinking we should elope."

"Good for him," Frank said.

"He'd never do that. Troy is a sensible boy." Myra seemed to be warming to this new idea. Then she switched tracks. "Emily should move back home. She must have spent all her savings by now and she still doesn't have a job."

"Yes, she does," Noelle said.

"Stacking books at the library? That's not a job."

"It's not?" Frank asked.

"She needs a real job and she's not going to get one this year. Nobody needs a high school mathematics teacher and that's all she's any good at."

"She can teach something else," Noelle said, defending her sister.

"Like what? She only knows math. She should have done a double major like you did. She needs to move back home."

"She likes to be independent," Frank said, unhelpfully.

Noelle set down her fork and sat up straight. "I'm independent."

"No, you're not. You're moving from your aunt's house to your husband's house."

"It's not just Aunt Myra's house. It's my house too."

"Of course it is, and it always will be, dear," Myra said, and then she spoiled the kind moment by adding, "I still don't see why we can't have the reception at the Country Club."

"Because, Aunt Myra, that's where Emily's reception was."

With a huff of exasperation, Myra asked, "What difference does that make?"

From the front door came the bang of the mailbox. The mailman had arrived with today's batch of Christmas cards and junk mail. Noelle went to collect it.

Frank and Myra stopped arguing, the doorknob Christmas bells rang, and the Labradoodle woofed, probably hoping for some attention. The rushing winter wind echoed all the way to the kitchen.

"I wish she'd change her mind," Myra said. "It would be lovely to have the reception at the Country Club."

"A lot cheaper to have it here." Frank poured himself more tea. "I like this stuff. You should make it more often." He added milk.

With her mouth open and an unspoken comment on her lips, Myra stared at him. "Oh well," she said. "At least the weather is cooperating. We'll have a white Christmas for the wedding."

"I doubt it." Frank looked out the bay window at the deep snow. "There's still over two weeks until Christmas Eve."

"It will be a white Christmas."

"Or what?"

"Don't be so pessimistic."

Noelle returned with a stack of mail and brought it to the dining room table. She sorted through the letters and cards and catalogs and as she did, she paused on one envelope. Then she picked up her poinsettia bag, tucked that envelope into it and pulled the drawstring.

"What is that, dear?"

"Uh, that brochure," Noelle said. "That brochure I wanted. For Hawaii. For the honeymoon."

"Can I see it?"

"I'll show you later," Noelle said. "I need to run some errands."

She looped the strap of her bag over her shoulder and took a step down the hall.

"Are you seeing your sister today?"

Noelle froze, looking like she was about to be caught. "Uh, why?"

"It won't take you a minute to drop by. I'll put some of these buns in a tin for her."

Assuming Noelle would visit her sister, Myra opened a tin—the blue one with the snowmen—and lined it with wax paper. She fit three buns inside the tin, snugged the lid and handed it to Noelle.

Noelle held the tin a moment, thinking, and then she set it on the bar and loosened the drawstring on her bag.

"Oh, Noelle?" Myra said. "I've decided to give you the crystal unicorn."

Noelle paused with her hand on the tin. Then she placed the tin in her bag and yanked the drawstring. "I'll be back later tonight," she said. "Don't wait up for me."

Chapter Four

Snow ending this evening
then cloudy with 60 percent chance of flurries

Making deep tracks in the snow, Emily trudged across the parking lot, pulling her scarf over her nose and lugging her bag of grocery essentials—milk, eggs, cottage cheese, two apples and a box of candy canes.

At precisely three o'clock this afternoon, yesterday's blizzard had returned, blasting the foothills city with arctic air and icy snowflakes. The sun had set at half past four, an hour before she'd left the library to take the bus home in the dark. In two weeks, winter solstice would give them the shortest day and the longest night of the year. Maybe by the time the days started to lengthen, her life would start to improve. If only something in her life could change.

Of course, something *had* changed, drastically. Meeting her former next-door neighbor in Las Vegas and marrying him within a matter of hours . . . that qualified as change.

She hadn't seen Mark since he'd helped her move last July. And until they'd met in front of Caesars on Saturday afternoon, she hadn't realized how much she'd missed him.

But to get married on the spur of the moment? In her whole life, she'd never done anything until she'd completely thought it out. How could she have married him?

Too much wine. Too much wine.

Besides, he was her *friend*. He wasn't marriage material.

Not the guy who used to have a different date practically every weekend.

Juggling the grocery bag and her purse, she fobbed her key card and let herself into the building. As she rode the elevator to her seventh floor apartment, her gloom deepened. She was twenty-five years old, an out-of-work mathematics teacher, and a disappointment to her aunt.

The library job didn't pay for the rent and her savings were almost gone. Much as she hated to admit defeat, she was going to have to move back home.

She let out a huge sigh. At least it really *was* her home. The will had left the Valley Ridge house to all three of them. Still, it felt like it was Aunt Myra's home. And Aunt Myra's rules.

If only there were a high school math teacher somewhere in Calgary who needed an immediate sabbatical.

Not likely to happen. It was more wishful thinking. She had to get over that, the wishful thinking. Things didn't happen because you wanted them to. A job was not going to suddenly appear. Not two and a half weeks before Christmas. The elevator eased to a stop and the doors silently slid open.

She turned left, rounded the corner and passed Mrs. Harcourt's door. Then she saw the box, and she stopped. The familiar box, long and cream-colored, waited in front of her apartment door. She had expected as much but it always felt like an invasion of her privacy that he could get into the building.

She walked the rest of the way to her door and set the grocery bag and her purse on the hall floor. Lifting the top off the box, she saw the roses—white ones. That was new. Usually they were red.

A tiny florist card peeked out between the long stems. It only said *Dan*. But that was all it ever said.

She dropped the card into the grocery bag and put the

lid back on the box. Then she retraced her steps to Mrs. Harcourt's door and knocked.

Half a minute later, Mrs. Harcourt answered, wearing one of her colorful long dresses. Emily presented her with the box.

"You lovely girl!" The old lady smiled as she lifted the lid. "White ones this time. Oh my!" Her rhinestone necklace sparkled in the light from the hall. "You know what that means."

"It means something?"

"White roses mean you want forgiveness. He wants you to forgive him, dear. That's progress."

No, it wasn't. It was practically a step backward. But she didn't tell that to Mrs. Harcourt. Instead she said, "I'm glad you like roses."

"I love them, dear. Now wait a minute. I have something for you." She took the roses inside, and returned with a round red casserole dish with a lid. "I was making Irish stew and I made a pot for you too."

Emily felt a glow wave down to her stomach as she thought about the food. *Real* food. "Thank you. That was very kind of you."

"You know I love to cook." The ringing of a phone sounded deep in the apartment. "That will be my daughter." Mrs. Harcourt said a quick goodbye and was gone.

With the heavy casserole dish warming her hands, Emily returned to her own door. At least Dan's roses gave her something to trade for all of this cooking.

Inside, she set down her armful, turned the oven on low and slid the casserole onto the middle rack.

After putting away her groceries, she noticed the little card on the floor. Dan's card. She picked it up and tossed it in the trash. And then she headed for the bathroom and a nice long bath.

. . . . .

With the winter tires crunching over the new snow, Mark drove into the Visitor Lot at Winward Groves and parked his SUV in the back row. Almost six-thirty. Emily would not have eaten yet, and if she had, she would have opened a can of tuna or something just as appetizing.

He cut the engine, put his head on the steering wheel and took a moment to think. Half an hour ago, he'd left the hospital but work buzzed in his head. Reports from the nurses. Results from blood tests. X-rays he'd signed off on. And, he still needed to call Pro.

He took out his phone and speed dialed Pro's number. He'd wanted to call sooner but there had not been a break in the day.

Pro answered on the first ring.

"She'll be fine," he told his friend.

A short pause, probably Pro registering relief. "Thanks for checking on her."

"She can be discharged tomorrow morning. Try to keep her off ladders." Knowing Aunt Tizzy, that would be difficult. The woman did not take direction well. "If you can, you'd better get over to her condo and decorate her tree for her."

"I've already booked off tomorrow," Pro said. "Have you talked to Emily yet?"

"I will," Mark answered. "Tonight. I don't think she'll be happy about the time this will take."

"That's the procedure. And rest assured, no one needs to learn about it."

They said goodbye and Mark got out of the SUV.

Light snowflakes fell on his cheeks. Maybe it would be a white Christmas. Or maybe not. It was only the seventh, over two weeks until Christmas, and by then they could have a Chinook.

The Chinook winds blew in from the Pacific coast, rose over the Rockies and dumped tons of snow on the ski resorts. After that, the dry wind descended to the prairie, sucking up moisture as it went, sometimes evaporating a foot of snow in a day and raising the winter temperatures.

The brisk wind ruffled his hair as he plowed through the deep snow and he wondered how hard it would be to convince Emily to go out to dinner. She couldn't afford restaurants and she wouldn't want him to buy. Maybe he could joke that it was their wedding dinner since they didn't have one in Vegas?

No, on second thought, better not.

He hadn't considered how he would approach this meeting. At the airport yesterday, she'd been upset, and distant. Not his usual Emily. At least, not the "before Dan" Emily. But they could handle this. They were two rational adults dealing with a slight mix-up. Except, they hadn't been so rational on Saturday night.

But they both had to eat and she'd want to know what Pro had said, so they might as well go over to the Keg. It wasn't like they were going on a date.

A nagging little voice in the back of his head said he could have phoned her. But it seemed better to discuss this in person. And besides, her camera had ended up in his luggage and he had to return it.

She'd snapped pictures everywhere they'd gone on Saturday night. Sometimes she'd handed the camera to a stranger, and then he and Emily had posed in front of the landmarks. Probably in front of every landmark in town.

He was looking forward to seeing the pictures but he hadn't had time yet. So he'd downloaded the card to his computer. Knowing Emily, she'd delete the card, sight unseen. As if she were deleting the night, making it like it had never happened. Because nothing happened in her life unless she planned it to the nth degree.

The whole thing was a mess, or it should be. When they were growing up, they'd spent so much time together and now . . . now, they didn't.

Somewhere along the way, they drifted apart. He'd been busy with his residency, she'd got engaged to Dan, and they never saw each other anymore. So, for whatever reason, he wanted to keep those pictures. He wanted to remember their night. Las Vegas had been a mistake, but it had been fun.

He'd almost reached the building entrance when out of the corner of his eye, he saw someone coming.

"Mark? What are you doing here?"

A woman's voice. Someone bundled up in a long blue coat, a blue knit hat and with a white scarf wrapped over her face.

"It's me. Noelle."

Of course it was. Emily's little sister. So much for a private discussion tonight. He should have recognized Noelle by the light blonde hair, the same color as Emily's. A few strands had escaped from Noelle's hat and the light blonde wisps danced in the wind as the snow swirled around them.

He did recognize the large carryall with the poinsettia stitched to the front. She'd had that on the plane yesterday. Today, a bottle of wine peeked out the top of the overloaded bag.

"I'm glad you're here," Noelle said. "I might need your help."

"My help?"

"Yes." She paused, gave him a puzzled look. Then asked again, "Why are *you* here?"

"I—I need to return Emily's camera. She forgot it on the plane."

"Good."

She could have meant it was good that he was here, or

that he was returning the camera, or that Emily had lost the camera in the first place. He hoped it didn't mean she wanted to see the pictures because that could be awkward. He pulled the entrance door open and held it for her. "Why do you need my help?"

"I have to talk Em into something," she said. "Have you had dinner?"

"Is that what's in your bag?"

"Sort of. I have Camembert and grapes and a great bottle of Chardonnay."

"Sounds promising." At least dinner sounded promising. But as far as helping Noelle talk her sister into something? He wouldn't be any help at all.

"I also have some cinnamon buns from Aunt Myra."

"Good ole Aunt Myra."

"She means well."

They always said that. "Maybe we can order out for pizza," he suggested.

As Noelle was taking off her mitts, he quickly hit the buzzer for Emily's apartment.

"Hello?" Her voice came over the intercom.

"It's Mark. And your sister is here too," he added, giving Emily a heads up. The door buzzed open and they entered, stomped off snow, and crossed to the elevator. "How is Aunt Myra?"

"As usual," Noelle answered. "She wants it to be a white Christmas."

"It might be."

"We're due for a Chinook. The snow will all be melted by Christmas." Noelle watched the numbers blinking out the floors. "You did get Christmas Eve off, right?

"Yes, Christmas Eve and Christmas Day."

"Perks of being chief resident?"

"Not really. I might get called in anyway. But don't worry, I'll be there for the ceremony," he told her. "At your house?"

"Yes. In front of the fireplace."

"Aunt Myra still trying to talk you into the Country Club?"

"Of course."

The elevator dinged open and they turned left. It was the first time he'd been here since he'd helped Emily move last July—two weeks after what would have been her wedding day.

The apartment door was propped open with her white boots, the rabbit fur Mukluks she'd bought last year because her feet were always freezing. Noelle pushed the door open. He followed her inside, grabbed Emily's boots and let the door close behind them. As he hung up his coat, he decided to leave the camera in his pocket and hope Noelle forgot about it.

A Celtic version of "Good King Wenceslas" was playing on her stereo, and he smelled the spicy aroma of something cooking.

Odd, because Emily didn't cook. Not in the past anyway. Maybe she'd learned for Dan. His gut tightened.

He pulled off his boots and headed to the little galley kitchen. She stood in front of the stove, under the bright overhead kitchen light. Her hair was wet and pulled back into a ponytail. She was dressed in faded blue jeans, a long sleeved green T-shirt and big gray socks. And she looked beautiful.

Beautiful? Why would he think that now? She always looked like this, beautiful. But this was different. This was a beautiful that made him want to touch her.

He closed his eyes and gave his head a shake. Must be a leftover feeling from the excitement of Vegas. Whatever it was, it would pass.

Emily donned a pair of red oven mitts.

A small bar divided the galley kitchen from the combination dining and living room. Noelle went to the other side of the bar and sat on one of the stools. There were no lights in the living room, and still no curtains or blinds, so the dark windows showed the black night.

Emily opened the oven and pulled out a large red casserole dish.

He moved closer. "You didn't make that."

"I can cook." There was a touch of defiance in her voice.

"Maybe," he said, "but you don't."

Standing next to her, he could see the brown stitching along the neckline of her T-shirt. The thread wove into a pattern of little pine cones. Her wet hair was making her T-shirt wet on the back. Again, he had that odd sensation of wanting to touch her, to touch her skin, right at the point where the wet T-shirt brushed the back of her neck.

She glanced up at him and smiled, a little shyly, with an awkwardness, something that had not been in their relationship before. But no matter, they would sort it out soon enough and everything would be back to normal. Forcing himself to move away from her, he went to sit beside Noelle.

"Mrs. Harcourt?" Noelle asked, as she set the bottle of wine on the bar.

"Yes," Emily answered. "Mrs. Harcourt. She made Irish stew this time."

Noelle unloaded a bag of grapes, a large round of Camembert and a blue tin decorated with snowmen. The tin would be Aunt Myra's cinnamon buns.

"More roses?" Noelle asked.

Roses? *More* roses? Mark looked from one woman to the other.

"Yes," Emily answered. "Dan doesn't give up."

Dan. Again. He clenched his teeth so he wouldn't say what he was thinking. Then he cleared his throat, attempted a casual, offhanded tone and said, "I didn't know you were seeing Dan again."

Emily rolled her eyes upward. "I'm not."

"Dan leaves roses outside Emily's door," Noelle told him. "And Emily gives them to her next-door neighbor."

This was news. "You give away the roses."

"I used to throw them in the garbage but Mrs. Harcourt likes them."

"How long has this been going on?"

"Since I moved here. Shortly after."

"Mrs. Harcourt is your next-door neighbor?"

"Yes."

"She's an old lady," Noelle said. "A little eccentric, but nothing serious. She likes to cook and she likes roses. And she keeps a spare key for Emily's apartment, in case Emily ever locks herself out."

Mark pressed his lips together. "Did you say he leaves the roses by your door?" Not good news.

"Yes."

He rubbed the back of his neck. "Your *apartment* door?"

"Yes," Emily said, as she lifted the lid from the casserole and steam rose up.

"How does he get in here? In the building?"

"I don't know. Somebody buzzes him up, I suppose."

"Don't worry about it, Mark," Noelle said, from her place beside him. "It's not like he's dangerous. He's just annoying."

"He shouldn't do that."

"What do you care, Mark?" Noelle asked him. "If I didn't know you better, I'd say you were acting like a jealous boyfriend. Now find us some glasses and a corkscrew."

"The door on the right." Emily pointed.

He looked and found a set of tumblers. "No wine glasses?"

"Nope."

"You got some for a wedding present."

"I did? How would you know?"

"I sent them."

"Oh," she said. "I'm not opening those presents. They're all still at Aunt Myra's house."

Not really Aunt Myra's house. Technically, the house belonged to all three of them. To Myra and Emily and Noelle but they all referred to it as Myra's house. Or rather, *Aunt* Myra's house. *Aunt Myra* wasn't *his* aunt, but he'd called her *Aunt* ever since his mother had left his father.

A faint ache pulsed in his chest with that memory, and then the feeling passed as quickly as it had come. He'd been nine years old and his mother had wanted a divorce. Of course, he was over that now.

"Emily wants to return the wedding gifts," Noelle said. "And the shower gifts. But Aunt Myra won't let her. She says Emily and Dan will get back together."

He looked into Emily's eyes, the clear blue eyes he knew so well.

"No," she said. And then dismissing the topic, she reached for some bowls. "Let's eat at the table in the living room."

Noelle glanced over her shoulder. "That's not a table, Em."

"It works."

Since there were only two stools at the bar, sitting around Emily's *table* sounded like a good idea. Emily handed Noelle a red tablecloth and Noelle took it to the overturned packing crate in front of the dark windows. She shook out the cloth, fanning it over top of the crate. The material smoothed over the wood and trailed onto the carpet.

Emily looked him in the eye again. "I'm still getting settled."

"Aunt Myra figures you'll give up and come back home," Noelle said, as she returned to the bar and the items she'd taken out of her carryall. "Any day now."

For sure, the apartment looked temporary. The two barstools were new, and maybe the only new furniture she'd added since moving day. The packing crate had held her stereo components—receiver, disk changer, speakers. He'd also helped her move a bed, a bedside table, linens, clothes, books, a small bookshelf, two cushions and a yoga bolster.

Right now, the cushions and the yoga bolster served as seats around the packing crate. The bookshelf stood in the corner near the windowed wall. Books crammed every shelf and more books were stacked on the floor. A piece of oddly shaped crystal sat on top of the shelves. In the dark, he couldn't make out what it was.

"What did you do with those candles?" Noelle asked.

"On the counter, next to the fridge."

Noelle found the two red pillar candles, each on its own silver saucer, and placed them on the tablecloth.

Five minutes later, the meal was spread out. Irish stew in the red casserole pot, the cinnamon buns in the snowman tin, a glass bowl of grapes, the cheese in the opened wrapper, and the wine.

Emily lit the candles and Noelle turned out the overhead light in the kitchen.

And then he could see out the windows. The building entrance, seven floors down, had a circular drive surrounding a cluster of evergreens lit up with blue and green and red lights. Someone had built a snowman beside one of the trees—two large balls and a much smaller ball for a head. The snowman had branches for arms and a scarf wrapped around its neck. From up here, he couldn't tell if it had a face. Snowflakes floated on the air, the storm lessening.

"Grab a cushion, Mark," Noelle said. "I'm starved."

Emily and Noelle sat across from each other. He sat

between them facing the windows, and the sky—the black velvet sky. No moon, no stars. The CD changer shuffled to a new disk, a trill of harp strings, and then an instrumental version of "We Three Kings of Orient Are."

"I like this," Noelle said. "Troy would like this."

Noelle didn't specify and could have been talking about the wine she was opening, or the aroma of the stew, or the soothing tempo of the music, or something else.

And right now, in this frozen moment of time, he liked . . . *this*, whatever it was. Simply being here, sitting at the table with Emily and her sister, listening to the soft Celtic Christmas carols, and watching the snow fall.

"Go on," Emily said. "Troy would like what?"

Noelle thought a moment. "The simplicity," she said. "He doesn't want a big wedding, and neither do I."

"Thirty people in the living room is not a big wedding."

"Not as big as what she had planned for you, but it's still big." Noelle's words seemed laced with resignation.

Emily ladled out stew for each of them. "It's hard to say no to Aunt Myra."

"She means well," Noelle said. "And we don't want to hurt her feelings."

Glancing over Emily's shoulder, Mark noticed the crystal piece on top of the bookshelves again. The candlelight wavered, reflecting off the crystal, making the object seem alive.

"What is that thing?"

Emily turned to see where he was looking. "Aunt Myra's unicorn."

"Oh," Noelle said. "I should tell you."

"What?"

"She wants me to have the unicorn."

Emily frowned and then her face smoothed and she shrugged. "That makes sense. It's for her first niece to get married."

"But I don't want it," Noelle said.

Emily waited a beat. And then, "Neither do I."

They both laughed.

Now that he knew what it was supposed to be, he could see it—a crystal unicorn, with the spike of a horn, the flare of a tail.

"Why does she want to give you a unicorn?"

"I don't know," Emily said, as she lifted a spoonful of stew to her lips and blew on it.

He let his gaze linger on her lips, remembered kissing her after the ceremony. A light quick friendly kiss. And then, when they were back outside the chapel, he'd kissed her again, longer that time. And she'd kissed him back, in a way no one had ever kissed him before.

They'd kissed many more times that night as they walked along the streets. Sometimes little kisses, sometimes longer, deeper kisses.

On the plane he'd told her he didn't remember because he didn't want her to feel embarrassed. That, and he didn't know what to make of the sensation it had stirred inside him.

But they'd been drinking. A lot. It would pass. He was sure of it.

"Mark?"

He did a double take. "Uh . . . what?"

"I said, would you like some cheese?" Noelle had cut the Camembert into wedges. "It's an impossible creature."

He had no idea what she was talking about.

It must have shown on his face, because Emily said, "The unicorn."

Right. They were still talking about that. He needed to pay attention. "Can't you tell her you don't want it?"

"No," they said together.

He didn't bother to ask. Where Aunt Myra was concerned, sometimes it was better not to know. They ate quietly for a few moments, listening to the harp strings.

"Mark?" Noelle got his attention. "Do you ever think about getting married?"

Cheese caught in his throat. He coughed. Twice. "Not usually," he said, avoiding looking at Emily.

"Why not?" Noelle persisted.

"Because it can only go downhill from there. First the marriage, then the divorce."

Noelle gripped her spoon, glared at him. "That's not what happens."

Crap. Foot in mouth . . . again. "Sorry. I didn't mean for you and Troy. I'm sure you'll be fine."

"But?" Noelle asked. "I know you were going to say something else."

He wasn't sure. "I don't know . . . . People leave." He shrugged, needing a subject change. Now.

"Not always," Noelle insisted.

"No, sometimes they just die," Emily said, surprising him with the wistfulness in her voice. And he surprised himself with the almost overwhelming desire he had to pull her into his arms and hold her.

Noelle sighed, dramatically, lifting her shoulders and puffing out enough air to stagger the candles. "It's Christmas, you guys! Do you have to be so gloomy?" She picked up the bottle of Chardonnay. "We need some wine."

"No," Emily said. "I've had enough wine to last a lifetime."

But Noelle filled their glasses. "We're celebrating," she said. "You need to let go more often, Em."

So they each held up a glass, clinking them together. The back of Emily's hand brushed against his. Normally, it would not have meant a thing. But tonight, his senses were on overdrive.

"To Christmas," Emily toasted.

"And to your new job," Noelle said.

"To my new job," Emily repeated.

They all clinked again and this time he was careful not touch her hand.

"I'm an advanced mathematics teacher who stacks books in a library," Emily said. "And you know what? I like it. It's relaxing. The staff are nice. And I like helping people find what they're looking for."

"But you like teaching," her sister said.

Emily gave a noncommittal shrug.

"You have a teaching job now," Noelle said. "I applied for you. The acceptance came in the mail today."

Emily stared at her sister.

"At Winward," Noelle went on. "Just down the road."

"Winward? Your school? And what do you mean you applied for me?"

"You wouldn't have applied yourself. Drink some of that wine."

"It's an elementary school!"

"Jannie, the ECS teacher, is pregnant and having problems."

"What?"

"Nothing that can't be helped by bed rest, so they need a mat leave replacement. Right away."

"I—" Emily sputtered. "I hope very much that she'll be okay, but did you say ECS?"

"ECS. Early Childhood Education."

"I know what it is!"

"Kindergarten," Noelle said, looking at Mark.

He started to laugh. "Kindergarten? Emily?"

"A bunch of rambunctious five-year-olds?" Emily was aghast.

"And I'll bet they're all unpredictable," he added, knowing how Emily liked predictable, and order, and no surprises. Same as he did.

"She can teach them to count," Noelle said. "How hard can it be?"

Chapter Five

Up on the housetop, click, click, click
Down through the chimney with good Saint Nick!

Emily waited in the office at Winward Elementary feeling like a student on detention. Four wooden chairs lined up next to the open door. She had chosen the chair closest to the door. In front of her was an inner office, the principal's office. The door was open but he wasn't there.

The rest of the main office was L-shaped. Emily sat at the base of the L, and the longer arm of the L held a small table with a coffeemaker and coffee supplies, then the secretary's desk, then a work table, and then the window.

The coffeemaker chortled as it brewed fresh coffee. A silver tray held ceramic mugs in various colors, a bowl of sugar cubes, non-dairy creamer and a carton of those little brown stir-stix.

Obeying the instructions on the sign by the school entrance, Emily had removed her Mukluks. She'd slipped on her indoor shoes and carried her boots to the mat outside the office. Her hat, scarf, mitts and purse were dumped on the chair next to her. The secretary had invited her to hang her coat on the coat stand beside the coffee table.

On the secretary's desk, an arrangement of fragrant evergreens and red carnations filled the room with a

Christmas smell.

"Coffee will be ready in a few minutes," the gray-haired secretary said in her high-pitched feeble voice. "Can I get you a cup?"

"No, thanks." Emily inhaled the aroma, wanting a cup of coffee, but there was no point in accepting it since she didn't intend to stay long enough to drink it.

Out in the hall, the babble of noise rose, the shouts and squeals and laughter. Compared to the hallway, the office was as calm as a yoga studio. Not a sound, except for the gurgling of the coffeemaker and the clicking of the stapler as the secretary organized some green booklets.

Outside the door a burst of commotion sucked Emily's attention back to the hallway.

"Oh good," Noelle said, sliding into the office. "I was afraid you'd chicken out."

"I said I'd come. But this is pointless."

Last night, Noelle had badgered her with arguments for why this was a good idea until finally Emily had promised she'd show up for the interview. But that was it. Only the interview. Once the principal realized she had no ECS experience, he would be crazy to hire her.

Out of breath, Noelle leaned on the door frame. "They'll love you."

"I'm unqualified. And now I have to work an extra hour at the library tonight."

"Don't worry about it." Noelle turned back for the hallway, and then stopped. "And what's up with you and Mark?"

Her nerves tightened. Had Mark told her? "What do you mean?"

"Last night. You looked like you were having an argument."

Aware that the secretary might be listening, Emily spoke quietly. "We . . . weren't."

"The body language," Noelle said, not lowering her voice. "It was loud and clear. You were trying hard not to touch each other."

Hoping the old secretary was hard of hearing, Emily forced a look of confusion onto her face. "It's your artistic temperament, Noelle. You're imagining things."

Stepping away from the door frame, Noelle stood tall. "I don't have an artistic temperament."

"Whatever temperament she has," the secretary said, "it suits her grade threes. No one runs a classroom like our Noelle."

"See?" Noelle smiled at her.

"You don't have a logical bone in your body," Emily said, hoping her sister would forget about Mark.

"Unlike you. You're full of logical bones." Noelle turned to leave, but stopped again. "I could pick you up after work and you could have dinner at home. Aunt Myra still does pizza on Tuesday nights."

Emily remembered with a pang of homesickness. "It's tempting." And it was, but listening to Aunt Myra's little hints about getting back together with Dan, that would be too much. And if Aunt Myra knew anything about this teaching position, there would be that to listen to as well. "Does she know about this job offer?"

"No. She saw me with the letter yesterday but I told her it was a brochure for Hawaii."

"Hawaii? You're going to Hawaii?"

"Honeymoon remember? We're supposed to have a honeymoon."

"Ah, yes." But, there was something about Noelle's tone. "You don't sound enthusiastic."

"Right now, it's just one more thing to do." Noelle bent down and hugged her. "I've got to go. The bell will ring in a minute." Noelle left, as quickly as she'd come.

One more thing to do? Emily slumped in her chair, feeling

like the world's worst sister. It sounded like Noelle was having reservations about the honeymoon. Was she having reservations about the wedding?

Emily hadn't noticed anything before. But then she'd been so immersed in her own problems with Dan—and now with Mark— that she hadn't spared a thought for her sister.

All the more reason to get this annulment over with and to do it as quickly as possible. If only she'd had a private moment to talk to Mark last night.

No doubt about it, commitments were confusing. Leaning her head back against the wall, she sighed, a deep audible sigh that the secretary must have heard.

"Are you sure you won't have some coffee?" the secretary asked. Then she fumbled her stapler and dropped it to the floor. Dipping over, her head disappeared behind the desk. A moment later she popped up again with the stapler. "It's hazelnut. The coffee," she said. "And it's really good."

"I'm fine," Emily answered, her tone firm enough to be convincing. She hoped.

But the fact was, she wasn't fine. She was worried about this awkwardness with Mark. And she was worried about someone finding out about the Las Vegas wedding. And, on top of that, she was worried about Noelle.

Finished with her stapling, the secretary stacked the pile of green booklets. "Mr. Valentine should be back inside any minute now."

Back inside? Had he gone to meet the buses for some reason?

The ancient secretary tottered over to the coffee pot. "He's with the Grade six class," she explained. "Some of them anyway. For igloo building."

Emily had been about to say *it's not a problem* or *I'm not in a hurry*, but—igloo building? Nobody built igloos in high school.

"It's extracurricular." The secretary poured coffee into a mug—a white ceramic mug painted with green holly sprigs and red berries. "With all the snow, Mr. Valentine thought someone might be interested." She shook in some dry creamer and stirred. "Turns out every student in walking distance wants to learn how to build an igloo. They all get here early, since they can't do it after school."

Why not? Emily thought. But she didn't say anything. However, her expression must have asked the question.

"It's too dark."

"I see," Emily said. "Yes, that makes sense." If anything made sense. Lately, not much did. Especially not that night in Las Vegas.

Too much wine. Too much wine.

She sighed. God, she hoped everything would just be done and over quickly. Before Aunt Myra found out. Because, somehow, Aunt Myra always seemed to find out.

And then there was last night. Noelle had shown up out of the blue, although that was the only way she ever showed up. Out of the blue. And Mark had arrived in person. What was that all about? Was there a problem with the annulment? Why hadn't he simply called liked he'd said he would?

With her sister there, Emily couldn't talk to Mark.

They couldn't talk. And they couldn't touch. And that was definitely awkward. No wonder her sister had noticed.

Emily felt another sigh coming on and quelled it before the secretary felt obliged to offer coffee again.

Then the school bell rang. Not a bell. Not like the old-fashioned teacher's bell that Aunt Myra had given her for graduation. This was the standard intercom version of a bell. The same as the bell at the high school where she used to teach. A harsh buzzer kind of sound. Fortunately, it only lasted a few seconds.

And then, music started to play.

Up on the housetop, click, click, click
Down through the chimney with good Saint Nick!

Behind the music, Emily could hear voices coming from the classrooms as the children joined in the singing.

"We do this every morning in December," the secretary explained. Choosing a large yellow mug with a smiley face on it, she poured coffee, added a dash of creamer and plopped in four sugar cubes. "The students love getting into the spirit."

As the secretary finished speaking, a tall man wearing an orange ski jacket and a red scarf barreled into the office. Mitts dangled from his coat sleeves, suspended by what looked like red yarn. The mitts were orange like his jacket. He also wore a Santa hat . . . and red and white striped socks. He must have left his boots on the mat outside the office.

"Good morning," he bellowed, apparently channeling his Santa persona.

"Good morning," Emily answered, wondering who he was.

The secretary handed him the steaming mug of coffee—the one she'd poured into the large yellow mug moments ago.

He wrapped both hands around it and looked thankful for the heat. "You must be the new recruit," he said. Then he took a sip of the coffee.

So, he was the principal. Emily picked up her purse and stood. "Emily Farrell," she said. "You must be Mr. Valentine."

"Call me Howie." He headed into his office. "Come on in."

She followed him. "I'm sorry to waste your time but—"

"Want some coffee?"

"No, thanks."

The Saint Nick song finished and an odd quiet descended. Mr. Valentine set his coffee on the desk and shrugged out of his coat. A second later he flung the coat, with its dangling mitts, over the top of the coat rack in his office. Next, he unwound the scarf from his neck and tossed it in the direction of the coat rack. He missed, and the scarf fluttered to the floor, landing next to a pair of moccasins—tan-colored, leather moccasins—one of them upside down.

"Mr. Valentine, there's something you should know right off the bat."

"Call me Howie." He took another sip of coffee, set the cup down, and then lifted the top file folder from a stack on the middle of his desk.

"I'm a math teacher," Emily said. "A high school math teacher."

Fanning the pages, he found what he was looking for, removed the sheet of paper and tossed the folder back on the pile. He picked up a coil bound agenda, and started turning pages. "Your sister speaks very highly of you." He was still wearing the Santa hat.

"Of course, she does. She's my sister." Noelle and Emily had always been close, and supportive of each other. And the thing about Noelle was she actually liked little kids. Emily, on the other hand, liked numbers. Numbers lined up in neat columns. Teaching senior high was where she needed to be. Helping students prepare for university entrance, that's what she was good at—and what she'd still be doing if she hadn't quit her job to go globetrotting with Dan.

What a mistake that was.

"Our Jannie had to go on mat leave early," Mr. Valentine said, as he made a notation in the agenda. He still hadn't sat down. Neither had Emily.

"That's what Noelle told me," Emily said. She rushed

on, wanting to get this interview over with. "I teach advanced calculus."

"That's nice."

"You do realize I don't have any ECS training," she said. "So you see—"

"But you are a teacher looking for work and, according to your sister, you're quite a good one."

"You don't understand. I can't—"

"Let's look at the classroom." He dropped the agenda on top of the file folders, shuffled into his moccasins, and headed out the door.

Emily glanced at the yellow mug of coffee, still steaming on the desk.

"Coming?" Mr. Valentine's voice boomed from the hallway.

It didn't look like she had a choice. At any rate, the fastest way to finish this interview was to go through the motions. He wanted to show her the classroom. So she would take a quick look and then she would leave.

Resigned, she looped her purse strap over her shoulder and turned to follow him.

Chapter Six

All is calm, all is bright

As Emily trudged after Mr. Valentine, one mantra played in her mind. *Waste of time. Waste of time.*

Sure she needed a teaching job. Sure she'd have to move back home because she didn't earn enough at the library to cover the apartment's rent. But there was no way she qualified for this position. And never mind the qualified part. She didn't *want* to teach ECS, regardless of how much she needed the money.

Three doors down from the main office, Mr. Valentine stopped outside a door decorated with white and blue sparkly snowflakes. Judging by the volume of noise radiating into the hallway, this was the kindergarten class. If he'd been expecting to impress her with how appealing the classroom and the class were, he'd failed miserably.

She still had no idea why they were even looking at the classroom. Mr. Valentine was supposed to ask her a few questions. He was supposed to find out how little she knew about teaching young children. And that would be mission accomplished. Noelle would get off her case and Emily would find a bus to the library and continue her day.

Mr. Valentine waited outside the door, either because he was afraid she'd run away, or because he was bracing before opening it. And then he opened the door and the wall of noise hit her. It was much worse than the earlier bedlam from the hallway before the bell rang.

And not only was it louder, it was a different quality of noise. The shouts and squeals were there, but ... no laughter. The laughter was missing.

Other sounds rose above the pandemonium—an adult shouting, and a child crying. It really was a child crying, and Emily couldn't handle a child crying.

Mr. Valentine stepped into the room and, reluctantly, Emily followed.

The door opened on the right side of the room. The opposite wall was the window wall. Stretching from three feet off the floor to the ceiling, the bank of windows illuminated the room with abundant light and showed a wintry white world outside.

To the left of the door, a row of multi-colored cubby lockers held coats and boots. Straight ahead, along the classroom's right wall, the large teacher's desk languished under the weight of piles of books and a jumbled mess of red and green papers. The teacher's chair was on the other side of the desk.

Along with the sounds of blocks toppling, and the shrieks and whoops and squawks, Emily heard the crying, coming from under the teacher's desk. A whimpering sound, like a lost kitten.

Beyond the desk, two miniature artist-type easels lined up next to the wall. One of them held a roll of paper at the top and Emily supposed the idea was to pull down a section of paper, paint on it, tear it off, and pull a new blank piece for the next child.

However, the four children gathered there did not seem to understand the concept. Together, they unraveled the roll of drawing paper, heaping it into a billow of white on the floor in front of the easel.

The other easel didn't have any paper, although it might have earlier this morning. One child stood in front of that easel. Using his fingers, he dabbed bright blue paint onto the wooden surface. Then he stood back, admired his work and wiped a blue streak over his red sweater.

"The ECS class has twenty-four children enrolled," Mr. Valentine said, speaking above the noise.

Even though he spoke loudly, no one seemed to notice them.

Other than the teacher's desk, there were no desks in the classroom. Instead there were three large child-size tables, each surrounded by eight child-size chairs. Two little girls sat at one of the tables, cutting strips of green paper. The other tables were abandoned.

Clusters of small children ranged about the room. On the far left side, in front of the cubbies, four children surrounded a wooden bin set up on legs. The legs made the bin high enough for the children to reach inside.

Using a pink plastic shovel, a little red-headed girl scooped up something white, and sprinkled it on the carpet. Another child joined her, doing the same thing.

"What is that white stuff?"

"Rice," Mr. Valentine said.

In front of the rice table was an area filled with large sturdy-looking cubes for climbing on. At least, that was probably what they were for, since six boys were crawling through them. Nearby, smaller blocks stacked in tall unsteady columns. The shiny plastic blocks and cubes ranged through a rainbow of vivid colors.

"We usually get parent volunteers to come in," Mr. Valentine said. "But at Christmastime, everyone is busy preparing for the holiday."

The first stack of blocks toppled and one of the boys dashed inside a cube, avoiding the crash.

In the midst of all the confusion, four children—two boys and two girls—chased around the room, randomly, as if they were pursuing a rolling ball that Emily could not see.

"Will you stand still!"

That was the adult, shouting from across the room, a woman in her mid-fifties, about Aunt Myra's age. The woman stood in the far left corner near the windows in an area defined by a yellow and green checkerboard mat. Behind her, piles of books cascaded from empty shelves into a heap on the floor.

Most of the woman's black hair was pulled back in a bun, but a few straggles had come loose and drooped around her face. She wore a three-piece business suit, dangling earrings, high heels, and smudged bright red lipstick. Gripping a little blond-haired boy, she tried to pull something purple and mushy out of his hair.

The child didn't seem particularly interested in having the purple stuff removed as he squirmed out of her hold.

"This is our current substitute," Mr. Valentine said. "She's a high school teacher, like you, except she teaches Social Studies, not Mathematics. When the board consolidated those two schools in the South, her position was lost and she had a choice between Junior High and ECS."

Emily and Mr. Valentine still stood near the door. The whimpering from under the teacher's desk had stopped, and Emily spied a little boy peeking at them through the slats under the desktop. His hair was dark brown. And his big brown eyes were open wide, tears on his eyelashes.

"She thought ECS would be easier," Mr. Valentine said. His shoulders slumped.

"Does she have ECS training?" Emily asked.

Mr. Valentine looked at her, his expression blank. "I don't believe so," he said.

"Mr. Valentine!" The teacher released the child, and he scurried away in the direction of the big plastic cubes.

"Hello, Mrs. Tadabousky. How are you today?"

"I cannot do this! I will not do this!"

"Not going well?"

"I don't care if it's only until Christmas. I can't stand it!"

Mrs. Tadabousky took a step toward them, and one of her heels sank into a ball of the soft mushy stuff, the same purple material she'd been removing from the boy's hair.

"I hate Playdough!"

Of course, that's what it was—Playdough. Emily vaguely remembered it from her own childhood. She'd never liked the way it smelled.

"I hate these kids! I hate that stupid reindeer song! And they let the gerbil loose!"

"The gerbil?" Mr. Valentine asked. "Where's the gerbil?"

"I have no idea!"

The distraught Mrs. Tadabousky stepped around two little girls who were drawing stick Christmas trees on a large sheet of craft paper on the floor. The branches of the trees glittered green with sparkle paint.

"Find someone else!" Mrs. Tadabousky shouted, and three seconds later, she exited the classroom.

Mr. Valentine took a deep breath and straightened his shoulders. "Emily?" he asked, using an even and calm voice. "Could you please wait here a few minutes while I deal with the substitute?"

Before Emily could answer, Mr. Valentine was gone.

So much for a quick interview.

She counted the students: five children at the easels, two at a table, four at the rice bin, two on the floor with the green sparkle paints, six on the cube toys, and four more darting about the room like a flock of swallows.

Plus, the little boy under the teacher's desk. All twenty-four present. And there was a gerbil somewhere.

Trying not to stare, she glanced at the boy under the desk again. He was still peeking through the slats. She thought she saw curiosity in his eyes.

Slipping her purse strap off her shoulder, she headed to the first cubby where she tucked her purse in the top shelf. Then she walked to the green and yellow checkerboard mat, kicked off her shoes and assumed a tree pose. The yoga balancing pose.

Mark always laughed at her when she did this, but it was a way of centering herself when she felt unable to cope with whatever was happening. Right foot grounded on the floor, left foot tucked up on her thigh, hands at heart center, eyes closed.

She focused on her breath, breathing evenly, feeling the air go in her nostrils and flow out again. *I know I'm breathing in. I know I'm breathing out.*

Around her, the room began to calm. The noise receded, like the tide rolling back, as gradually her brain made the room silent.

Or, was the room really silent?

She opened her eyes, and saw twenty-three children gathered around her, all attempting the tree pose. Some quite proficient, some wobbly. All trying. All quiet.

She sat on the checkerboard mat, lotus pose. So did they. Again, mimicking the pose. From under the teacher's desk, the little boy watched.

"Breathe in through your nose," she said. "In and in. Hold it." She paused. "And now out through your mouth—with an ahh."

A room full of ahhs followed.

They did another breath in and another out, then she said, "Now we will hum when we breathe out."

A few seconds of silence while they inhaled, and then the room hummed like a swarm of bees.

She wasn't sure where to go from there, so she left it to them. The little red-headed girl, the one who'd been sprinkling the rice, spoke first. "Are you the new teacher?"

"Will you stay?" another child asked.

"Where's Mrs. Jannie?"

"Did she die?"

The questions stopped after that last one, and Emily watched the somber little faces. The blond-haired boy, the one with the purple Playdough in his hair, said, "Did we kill her?"

Odd questions, Emily thought. "No, you didn't kill her and she didn't die. She just needs a rest."

"Is she sick?"

"Why is she sick?"

"Is she going to die?"

They were in kindergarten. What was it with all this death stuff? "Mrs. Jannie needs a rest. It happens sometimes when a woman is having a baby."

They thought about that and then the boy with the blue paint on his sweater said, "My mom says Mrs. Jannie is under whelmed."

"I think she means overwhelmed," Emily said.

"Yep. *Over* whelmed," the child agreed.

A space of silence followed and then Emily asked, "What do you do first thing in the morning?"

"Mrs. Jannie lets us do whatever we want." This from the little red-headed girl again.

"Play on the big toys," from two of the boys at the same time. They looked alike, probably fraternal twins, the same clothes, but one in blue, one in red.

"Color," from one of the girls who'd been making the Christmas trees with the green sparkle paints.

"Paint," from the boy in the red sweater with the blue swipe of paint across it.

"Playdough!" The red-headed girl answered again. "That stuff in Kyle's hair," she explained. "That's Playdough. My mom made it. We put in purple food color."

"I see." Emily made eye contact with the girl, nodded,

and then moved her attention to the rest of the group. "I understand there's a gerbil in here."

That had them giggling again.

Afraid that control would be lost, Emily folded her hands at heart center. "Everyone breathe in."

They followed suit, apparently liking imitation.

"Hold it," she said. "Now, ahh."

A roomful of ahhs.

Order restored, the next step would be finding the gerbil. That was as good a start as any. "If you have some cheese in your lunch bag, put your hand up."

Four hands shot up, including the red-headed girl. And then after a moment, another three hands.

Ignoring Red, and the others who had already spoken, Emily pointed to the child across the circle. "What's your name?"

"Kelly."

"What kind of cheese do you have?"

"String cheese."

"Good," Emily said. She pointed to another child. "What's your name?

"Allison," the girl answered. "What's *your* name?"

Good question. Of course they'd want to know who she was. Even if she wasn't staying. "Emily."

"No, it's not," the child said.

"It's not?"

"It's Mrs. Emily because you're the teacher."

"I see." Although, she was not a Mrs. yet. Technically she was, but not really. "Let's go with Miss Emily. Now, what kind of cheese do you have?"

"I have orange cheese."

"Is it cheddar?"

"I don't know. It's orange."

Emily pointed to a third student. "What's your name?"

"Bobby. And I have monster cheese," he said.

Could be the French Munster cheese, probably a bland variation. "Kelly, Allison, and Bobby. I want you to pretend to be elves. Find your lunch bags, and bring a piece of cheese to me."

The three children tiptoed away in a competition for quietness. Pretty competitive for kindergarten, but was this where it started? This competitiveness. Never mind, she had to find the gerbil.

"Where is the gerbil's cage?" she asked.

"We hid it under the books," the blue twin said.

"Of course you did." Emily looked at the heap of books in front of the empty bookshelves. "What's the gerbil's name?"

"Chewy."

"Chewy."

"Chewy!"

"Chewy!"

"Chewy!!"

Emily folded her hands at heart center. So did they, and the chatter faded. When the room was quiet again, she said, "Do you think Chewy misses his cage?"

There wasn't an immediate answer. They looked thoughtful, and some of them looked . . . *sad?* Then the boy with the blue streak of paint across his red sweater said, "Did we kill him?"

Chapter Seven

Frosty the Snowman

Dr. Mark Bainbridge retreated to the staffroom, silently giving thanks to the person who had made a fresh pot of coffee. It was almost noon. Nine hours without a break.

He'd left Emily's last night around ten, because it didn't look like Noelle was leaving. At least not until she'd talked Emily into an interview, and Emily would never agree. She liked things organized and it was doubtful she'd find that in a kindergarten classroom.

Fortunately, he'd gone straight to bed, because he'd been paged at three this morning and things had not slowed down since.

He filled one of the hospital white ceramic mugs, added creamer and sat at the small table next to the window. The patio was covered in snow again and someone had built a snowman—decorated with a surgical cap, a tongue depressor mouth, medicine cup eyes and a roll of adhesive tape for a nose. A red stethoscope acted as a scarf around Frosty's neck and a surgical mask dangled below that.

Sipping his coffee and looking out the window at Frosty, Mark felt like . . . well, anything but a jolly happy soul. He couldn't seem to muster the Christmas spirit everyone was feeling. In fact, he wished he could skip over the holidays altogether. He ran a hand through his hair, tilted his head from side to side to get out the kinks.

It was the hours . . . the long hours. That had to be it.

No, he was used to that. In fact, he thrived on it. He liked dealing with broken bones. He could fix broken bones.

So . . . was it Judith? She'd phoned last night, right about the time he was leaving Emily's apartment. He'd ignored the call, because he hadn't known what to say. And then he'd muted the phone.

He hadn't got in touch with her, not since Vegas. Naturally she'd expect a call. She probably assumed he was busy at the hospital, and for the most part, he was. He sighed and stared at Frosty, watching the crystal snowflakes glint in the sunlight. Frosty stared back at him, the tongue depressor mouth giving him a stern expression.

No, Judith wasn't the problem. Not really. When the time came, he'd deal with Judith. Or maybe he'd be ready to see her again. Anyway, it had been almost a month since they'd been on a date. She was busy with her accounting practice and year-end issues. He had December issues . . . skiers on early season slopes hitting rocks . . . people falling off rooftops stringing up Christmas lights.

He set his mug on the table and dropped his head into his hands. He knew what was wrong. The thing that was messing with his mind was Emily.

He didn't like that she was short of money. And he didn't like that she might have to move back home with her Aunt Myra. And he sure as hell didn't like the way Dan was sneaking into her building and leaving flowers outside her door.

You weren't there for her, Frosty seemed to say. A sudden gust dusted over the patio, creating little whirlwinds in front of the snowman.

It wasn't my fault, Mark told himself. She went to university. She met Dan. She fell in love with that idiot.

Mark closed his eyes, inhaled the smell of the steaming

coffee, and realized it wasn't the standard hospital issue. Kit Livingston hated the hospital coffee and sometimes brought in his own special blend. This was the special stuff, and Mark appreciated it. He took another sip, savoring the flavor.

He and Emily had been best friends for as long as . . . . Well, it had started when he'd been in grade four and she'd been in grade one.

He was alone, except for the nanny and the nanny didn't care about him. Sometimes it felt like his dad didn't care either, but in fairness, the divorce had hurt his father, too. So when six-year-old Emily had seen him sitting on his front steps, she'd taken his hand and brought him home. And for the next three years, Emily's mom had treated him as if he was one of her own kids.

After the accident, it wasn't quite the same. But by then Emily was like a sister to him, so he still went home with her after school every day. Eventually Aunt Myra accepted he would be there. Of course, Emily would not have it any other way.

And then Myra got pneumonia, was admitted to hospital, and Emily and Noelle went into foster care. That was a stressful, terrible time. Finally their aunt was well enough to come home, and Emily and Noelle came home too. And once again, he went to their house after school. Every day.

He needed to talk to her. Tonight. To let her know what Pro had said, about it taking a year. And to reassure her that no one would find out about it.

Except, he couldn't talk to her tonight. He was on call tonight. *Damn.* He gulped more of Kit's special blend and watched the snow swirling around Frosty. He could call her during a break. No, that would be bad. He needed time to explain, and he needed to do it in person.

Okay, he could wait and see her tomorrow. Also bad. It

wasn't fair to make her wait so long. She was anxious to know what was going on. She'd said as much. And she was right.

Kit? Maybe he could get Kit to cover for him? Why not? The guy owed him from last week. And it wasn't like Mark asked for a lot of favors.

But would Emily be home? What if she had other plans?

She'd be home. She had to be. Because he needed to see her. And once he'd told her about needing a divorce—not an annulment—and about the timing for the divorce, he could mention, casually, that she couldn't marry Dan, no matter what. Not until at least a year had passed. That was the silver lining to this cloud.

"What are you grinning about?" Holding a chart and a bunch of X-rays, Kit stood next to the table, almost as though he'd been summoned.

Mark smiled. Good fortune had finally decided to show up. "Dr. Livingston," he said, lifting his cup to his friend.

"Dr. Bainbridge," Kit answered as he took a seat and got right to the point. "I wanted to talk you about that skier they flew in from Sunshine. Have you seen his X-rays?"

"I saw them. Completely torn ACL."

"Yeah," Kit said. "I think he's a good candidate for a reconstruction."

"He's not a professional?"

"No, but he's young and he's a devoted amateur. He'll want to ski the bumps again."

They both knew it was a complicated surgery, and a long recovery. "Make sure he understands what he's in for."

"I will. I'll get started on the workup right now." Kit got up.

"Uh, Kit?"

"What?"

"Can you cover for me tonight?"

A slight pause. "Sure," Kit said. He waited a couple more seconds, and then, "You must have had a good time in Vegas. Did you meet someone?"

"No," Mark answered. "I . . . uh . . . need some sleep, that's all. I've been here since three this morning."

"Whatever you say." Kit didn't ask any more questions. A moment later he was gone.

One problem solved. Now to phone Emily.

Mark reached in the pocket of his lab coat, retrieved his cell and spotted the readout.

One new message.

He'd missed it, since the phone was still muted from last night. Had Emily tried to get in touch?

Feeling his spirits lift, he turned the volume back on and swiped the screen.

Nothing from Emily, but his dad had left a message, and Frank Bainbridge rarely left messages. His dad had only recently discovered texting, and mostly he hated cell phones. The guy would sooner send a letter than a text, so the fact that he was sending one now meant he had something important to talk about.

Clicking on the text icon, Mark found his father's message.

Call home.

That was it, but at least it was a message. A quick tap to the screen and the call went through.

After the third ring, Frank Bainbridge answered. "You got my text?"

"Just now. I had—"

"How come it took so long? I thought text was supposed to be fast?"

"It is, but—"

"How about coming over tonight for pizza. Homemade pizza."

Homemade pizza? "You're making pizza?"

"Of course not. Myra is making pizza. It's Tuesday night."

Yes it was. An old tradition. And any other time, pizza might have been nice. Except tonight he wanted to see Emily. In the background, he could hear the Labradoodle bark. Makita probably wanted to go for a walk.

"Noelle said Emily is coming," his father told him.

Emily? That was good. Except . . . he wanted to see her alone, not with a crowd.

"You should come too." His dad persisted. "You hardly ever come home."

Mark pulled the phone from his ear and stared at it. If he hadn't known better, he might have thought his dad missed him.

Making a decision, he got back to the conversation. "Sure," he said. "I'll be there."

At precisely twelve o'clock, the school bell rang. Or rather, the buzzer sounded. That buzzer noise seemed appropriate in the high school, but not here. Not in kindergarten. Why couldn't somebody invent a computerized version of a school bell?

Francine, the little redheaded girl, provided her next piece of instruction. "Now we get our lunches and we sit at the tables."

At the high school there was a cafeteria, but not at Winward Elementary. Here, everyone brought their lunch to school. Emily wished she had brought hers.

"The older kids go to the lunchroom but we're not mature enough for that," Francine said. "So we have to eat here. Then we play outside."

Taking the child's advice, Emily said, "Okay. Everyone go to your table."

They all stopped what they were doing, the room fell silent, and then they rushed for the tables, as if this were a game of musical chairs. Except they each went to their specified chair.

They settled quickly and waited to hear what she'd say next. "I want table one to get up first and get your lunches."

Once again, as if it were a competition for quietness, the children quickly headed for their cubby lockers, making as little commotion as possible.

At precisely that moment, Noelle showed up at the door balancing four mandarin oranges in one hand. She did a double take, looking like she'd come into the wrong room. And then, she approached the teacher's desk where Emily stood.

"Hi," Noelle whispered.

"Hi," Emily whispered back.

Noelle stared at the children, then focused on the center table. "Francine, Hannah, Jillian, Joanne." Still whispering, she frowned. "Katie, Keith, Kelly, Kyle."

Her sister taught grade three, but she knew the children's names in this room. Impressive. But why was she frowning?

By this time, the table one students had returned to their seats. "Table two," Emily said out loud, and eight children eased out of their chairs and tiptoed to the cubbies.

"Oh my God." Noelle started to laugh. And then speaking out loud she said, "You alphabetized your students?"

"I had to learn their names in a hurry."

Noelle thought about that for a second and then handed two of the oranges to Emily.

"Miss Emily? Table three?" Francine prompted her.

"Yes, table three."

The last group headed for the cubbies, collected their lunches and returned to their seats. As they opened their lunches, the room gradually filled with a normal level of chatter.

"How come they're so quiet?" Noelle asked, as she peeled one of her oranges.

"They're worried about the gerbil. They don't want to disturb him."

"Ahh," Noelle said. "I heard about the gerbil. Did you find it?"

"We put his cage behind the easels, put some cheese in there, and left the door open."

"He came back to his cage?"

"He came back," Emily said.

"And the quiet seems to have stuck." Noelle looked at the students sitting around the three tables. "Where's Benjy?"

Emily pointed down. "Under the desk. He's sitting on one of those fuzzy sheepskin mats. He seems comfortable enough so I'm letting him be."

Noelle nodded. "Mrs. Tadabousky tried to drag him out. That didn't go over well."

Picturing that, Emily had a flash of dislike for the old teacher. But why was the child hiding from Mrs. Tadabousky? Emily was about to ask her sister when one of the twins approached. The red one, Keith.

"This is for Benjy," he said, holding what looked like a peanut butter and raisin sandwich.

"Does he have a lunch in his cubby?"

"Yes, but he won't eat it. He likes peanut butter."

A small hand reached out from under the desk and accepted the peanut butter sandwich.

"What are you going to eat?" Emily asked.

"I have my own sandwich," Keith said. "My mom made that one for Benjy."

Good for Keith's mom. At least someone seemed to understand what was going on with Benjy. Emily broke off a wedge of her mandarin and wondered if Benjy liked mandarin oranges. She held it beside the desk.

The little hand reached out and accepted the piece of orange.

"I can't believe you alphabetized your students." Noelle peeled her own orange.

"They're not my students."

"Not technically. Not yet."

"What do you mean?"

"Mrs. Tadabousky went home, and I don't think she's coming back. She said something about an early retirement."

Emily broke off another piece of the orange and passed it under the desk. And Benjy accepted it.

She wished she knew what was going on with the boy. There had to be a reason he was hiding. But this wasn't her problem. And it wasn't even a problem she knew how to deal with. She had to get on with her day. And at some point she had to get in touch with Mark and find out how long it was going to take to get out of this marriage.

Awkward, but she had to deal with it. "Do you know what's up with Mr. Valentine? I can't stay here all day. I have to get back to the library."

"I phoned to let them know you might be late," Noelle said.

"Late? I was supposed to be there two hours ago."

"Don't worry about it." Noelle cradled the orange wedges in her hands. "Do gerbils eat cheese?"

Cheese? Emily eyed her sister who was obviously changing the subject. "I googled it on my phone," she said. "Small quantities are okay."

"That's a good start. Finding the gerbil."

Perhaps. Emily thought about that. "Now they're afraid they'll upset it and it will die. That's why they're being so quiet. What is it with these kids and death? Is that a TV thing?"

Just as Noelle started to answer, the classroom door swung open. Mr. Valentine entered, wearing his Santa hat and a hopeful expression. He surveyed the room, and approached the teacher's desk. "The job is yours," he said. "If you want it."

"But," Emily stammered, "I'm not qualified." She glanced under the desk. Not only not qualified, but she had no idea of what to do with Benjy.

"There's yogurt in the staff fridge," Noelle said.

"Yogurt?"

"You didn't bring any lunch, did you?"

In the end, after checking with her supervisor at the library, Emily agreed to stay . . . at least until Christmas. Mrs. Klaus, the library supervisor, told her to take her time with deciding. She also said that Emily could come back to the library after Christmas if kindergarten didn't work out.

The blue twin, Brian, had given Emily the sandwich from Benjy's lunch box. Apparently, Benjy did not like roast beef sandwiches and that is what he got, every day. And every day, he simply threw the sandwich in the trash. "You can eat it," Brian told her. "Benjy says he wants you to have something to eat."

So Emily ate the offered sandwich, and enjoyed it, especially the tangy Dijon mustard—which was probably a taste Benjy had yet to acquire. Whoever made his lunch did not seem to understand what the child liked to eat.

Noelle helped the children get dressed to go outside and play. After lunch, there was a story followed by nap time, followed by more questions about Chewy's health and the possibility of him dying.

And then the school day ended.

Keith and Brian, the twins, seemed to be looking out for Benjy, and they took the same bus home. Keith brought Benjy's coat to him and Brian brought his boots.

After a flurry of coats and mitts and hats and boots, the twenty-four children were gone and the room was silent, except for Chewy running laps on his gerbil wheel.

"You did well for your first day." Her sister had reappeared.

"I still don't think this is a good idea. I'm a math teacher, not an ECS teacher."

"You can learn."

Emily and her sister spent the next two hours loading paper onto the easels, refilling paint pots, stacking books, wiping tables, collecting blocks, and clearing off the teacher's desk, where Noelle found Mrs. Jannie's Teacher Planner—with its page that listed the names of the students.

"How did you alphabetize them if you didn't know their names?" Noelle asked, eyebrows raised.

Emily shrugged. "It was easy. Some of them know how to print their name. Everyone has their name written on something. A book or a backpack. So I knew how to spell Hannah with an "h" at the end. And Jillian with a J."

"Not bad for an advanced mathematics teacher. I thought the only practical thing you could do was count."

"Like you're practical?"

"Of course I am," Noelle said. "Now we need to eat. Let's go and get some of Aunt Myra's pizza."

Emily grimaced.

"Don't say no. There's nothing in your fridge."

"Yes, there is."

"The casserole is all gone. There's some cottage cheese

and candy canes. That's it. So unless your next-door neighbor has cooked you something, which would not happen two nights in a row, you're coming home for pizza."

Chapter Eight

A mix of sun and cloud. Clearing this evening.
Wind southeast, becoming light.

At seven o'clock, Mark and his dad and the Labradoodle walked next door to Myra's house. The latest storm had passed, and the temperature had risen. Still below freezing, but mild compared to the last few days.

"Should we be bringing Makita?"

"I always do."

Myra would freak if the dog jumped up on her furniture. "Are you sure she won't—"

"As long as you're not bringing another new girlfriend, she won't mind."

Mark looked away. Myra had always objected to the girlfriends he'd brought home. All of them.

But that was Myra, always interfering—and maybe she did mean well, but still.

He hadn't seen her in a long time, not since the failed rehearsal dinner last June. "It doesn't matter what I do," Mark told his father. "I never make her happy."

"Keep trying."

They'd reached the front door and, like the old days, they simply walked in. A strand of Christmas bells on the knob jingled as the door opened. His dad looped Makita's leash over the knob on top of the bells and the dog curled up on the mat.

"Come to the kitchen, Frank," Myra shouted from the back of the house, and then she appeared in the hallway. "I need some help with—oh!" Holding a dish towel in her hands, she came to a halt and frowned at him. And then she said, "Hello, Mark." It was a cool hello, and not particularly welcoming.

So. His dad had invited him without telling Myra. Interesting, and gratifying. His dad really did miss him. Considering how his dad rarely showed affection, that felt good.

"Hello, Aunt Myra," Mark said. "Nice to see you." He grinned at her, knowing she was not happy to see him.

It didn't matter. He was here because of Emily. And later, he would get her alone in the backyard. He'd build a fire in the fire pit. That would work. Emily liked having fires out there, especially in the snow. They'd done that quite often, sitting on the old lawn chairs wrapped up in blankets. And, as darkness fell, they'd watch the stars come out and talk until the embers burned low.

The doorbell rang behind them and his pulse jumped. *Emily.* He moved Makita and her leash aside and, smiling, opened the door.

Not Emily. His smile fell away and, belatedly, he realized she would not have rung the bell.

"Dan?" he said, exuding the same amount of warmth that Myra had used a moment ago. "What are you doing here?"

"I was invited," Dan said, unbuttoning his coat.

The guy stood there, with his stylish hair, his ironed shirt, and his smug expression. "What are you doing here?"

"He was invited," Mark's dad said, as if it were true.

Dan slipped out of his boots, then shrugged off his coat and handed it to Frank. "Hi, Mr. Bainbridge."

And that was it. The idiot left them at the door and trotted down the hall toward the kitchen—and Myra—as if he were her trained puppy.

The bells jingled again and the door opened a second time. Noelle stepped inside followed by Emily, who wore a long red coat, a red knit hat and a white scarf. Strands of her pretty blonde hair escaped the hat and dusted over her face.

Her eyes lit up when she saw him. "Mark! I didn't know you were coming."

"I knew you were."

She looked confused. He leaned closer to her and, in a low voice, he said, "Don't go ballistic. Dan is here."

Her mouth fell open and she turned to look at her sister.

Noelle raised her shoulders in a gesture that said, *don't blame me.*

His dad was still at the door, holding Dan's coat. Frank dropped the coat on the floor and helped Noelle get out of her coat.

"It wasn't Noelle," Mark said. "I think it was Myra."

"I can't handle this. I'm leaving."

"No," he caught her arm. "We'll work with it."

"But—"

"Remember when we used to build fires in the snow?" He put his arm around her shoulders and hugged her to him. "Play along," he said.

Once the coats were in the closet—except for Dan's coat, which Makita was sitting on—they all joined Dan and Myra.

"Great weather," Frank said, arriving in the kitchen first.

"What do you mean? Great weather?" Myra frowned.

"I mean it's stopped snowing, the roads are good and it's not freezing cold. And the moon is in the last quarter and almost gone, so we might be able to see the northern lights."

His dad had always loved watching the sky. It was the one thing they did together. Mark had forgotten about that.

"We need snow," Myra said. "We need a white Christmas for the wedding."

Frank glanced up at the ceiling, shaking his head. "It's not like you can order the weather, Myra." He opened the fridge. "Got any beer?"

The Aunt Myra that Mark knew didn't drink beer. But his father had found a bottle of Rickard's Red. And he knew where the opener was. That was a new development.

Noelle, on the other hand, preferred wine. With a bottle of Chardonnay under her arm, she rummaged through a kitchen drawer and retrieved a corkscrew.

A granite counter divided the kitchen from the dining room. Mark walked around the counter, sat on one of the stools and watched the activity in the kitchen. Emily sat beside him, silent. And vigilant.

He wanted to put his arm around her, like he had at the door. But that didn't seem like a good idea. Not if they were going to keep their . . . marriage . . . a secret. Because right now he wasn't sure he could pull off a brotherly hug.

Whoa. Where had that thought come from?

From nowhere, he decided. It wasn't like he had romantic feelings for her. But he did have protective feelings for her. And he didn't like the way Dan was staring at her, like she was guilty of some horrible crime.

Dan strolled over to the fridge and got a beer for himself. Also Rickard's Red.

"Noelle," her aunt said, as she opened the oven. "I asked Dan if he would be Troy's best man."

The corkscrew slipped out of Noelle's fingers and clattered onto the counter. Gripping the wine bottle with both hands, Noelle closed her eyes and appeared to be steadying herself. Then she said, "Have you asked Troy?"

"Troy will do what you tell him."

Noelle picked up the corkscrew and fit it into the bottle. "No, he won't." The corkscrew twisted in. "Troy's friend Jeff is the best man."

"Jeff can be a groomsman."

"Is Troy coming tonight?" Dan asked, as if he were trying to change the topic, or move on from it.

"He has to work late," Noelle answered.

"Dan is the perfect choice," Myra said to no one in particular.

With the oven open, the aroma of sausage and tomatoes and spices escaped into the kitchen. Mark's mouth watered.

"It will be wonderful having Dan and Emily together in the wedding party."

Together? Myra was still trying to salvage that engagement? Mark pressed his hands hard on the granite countertop. His muscles tensed as he glanced at Dan again. The guy looked so sure of himself . Was it possible Emily wanted to get back together with that idiot?

"It's the best way to—"

"Myra." Frank stared at her, eyes brooking no argument. That one word might have meant stop, or reconsider, or this is none of your business. Whichever it was, his intent was clear.

"You stay out of this, Frank. You don't understand how women think."

"I'm sure we can come up with a workable solution," Dan said, in a feeble attempt to be helpful.

Still sitting at the counter, Mark pulled in another long, deep breath. He hadn't known Myra was still pushing for Emily to marry Dan. And he hadn't known how Myra's constant needling affected Emily.

But he should have. For the whole time they'd been growing up, Mark had watched Emily and Noelle cater to their aunt's wishes. Most of the time they'd gone along with those wishes, because Myra was easier to live with when she had her own way.

But choosing Troy's best man? That was pushing it, even for Myra.

Noelle set a glass of wine in front of Emily. She reached to take it, but her hand was shaking. So she used both hands to steady the glass and took a quick drink.

This was probably the first time she'd seen Dan since the rehearsal dinner. Maybe leaving would have been a better idea.

But, on second thought, maybe it was good to get this meeting over with. She had to face Dan sometime.

As Mark had that thought, Dan sauntered out of the kitchen, around the counter, and into the dining room where six chairs surrounded the old oak table.

Mark spun on his stool and watched the guy claim the end chair.

Dan sent him a hard glance, a proprietary look, as if he were challenging Mark's right to be here. Challenging his right to be sitting beside Emily.

Emily picked up her glass and moved into the kitchen, so Mark followed her. It was time for a beer anyway. He looked in the fridge, saw four bottles of Rickard's Red and took one.

By the time he opened it, Myra had sliced the pizza. She set the tray on the table on top of a wooden board and Mark licked his lips. Simply by breathing in, he could almost taste the medley of sausage and tomato and cheese and little bits of red peppers. He hadn't known he was so hungry.

"Emily," Myra said, "you sit here, beside Dan."

Emily stood frozen in her corner of the kitchen, but Noelle approached the table, with her wine glass in one hand and the opened bottle of Chardonnay in the other. She took the place by Dan, sitting on the long edge of the table with her back to the windows. She positioned the wine bottle and her wine glass in front of her plate.

With the chair next to Dan occupied, Emily came around the counter and sat beside her sister.

Mark chose the seat at the head of the table, next to Emily. His father sat beside him. And Myra sat next to Frank in the last place, so she had Frank on one side and Dan on the other.

From here, Mark could see across the counter into the kitchen and, in the other direction, the glowing gas fireplace and the dark windows.

The windows showed a reflection of them all sitting around the table. If it had still been daylight, he would have been able to see the fire pit in the backyard, assuming it wasn't buried under snow.

They each helped themselves to their first slice. Perhaps the best pizza he'd ever tasted—bursting with flavor, dripping with tomato sauce and oozing cheddar cheese. Myra's cooking almost made up for her interfering.

Almost.

After a few minutes, Myra started up again. "You know what I think?" she said. "I think the best man needs to be—"

"Emily has a new job." Noelle blurted that out.

Unlikely, Mark thought. Emily would not have taken that kindergarten job. This was Noelle's attempt to get Myra off the best man topic.

Myra frowned. "A new job?"

Noelle had quickly polished off her first slice of pizza. She reached for a second piece, plopped it onto her plate and picked off a piece of red pepper.

Myra prodded. "A . . . teaching job?"

Emily had eaten half of her slice. Now she didn't seem hungry. "It's only for two weeks," she said, sounding apologetic. "Only until Christmas."

She'd taken the job? He hadn't expected that. But then, it wasn't as if a two-week stint was a commitment.

"Where?" Myra asked.

"At my school," Noelle said. She gulped some wine. She also seemed to have lost her appetite. Her second slice of pizza languished on her plate, minus a few pieces of red pepper.

"At Winward Elementary?" Myra frowned. Paused . . . her fork in the air. "Emily is teaching at an *elementary* school?"

"ECS," Noelle said, setting down the wine, seeming calmer.

"ECS?" Myra's voice squeaked.

"Kindergarten," Mark told his father. He still wasn't sure this was true. How could Noelle have talked Emily into kindergarten? *Emily?* The person who couldn't stand if a little kid happened to cry. It made no sense.

"Never had kindergarten when I was growing up," Frank said, sliding another slice of pizza onto his plate.

"But Emily is an advanced mathematics teacher!"

"Teaching is teaching," Noelle said.

"She can't teach ECS!"

"She did a good job today. And the school is in walking distance of Winward Groves," Noelle said. "She won't have to take the bus."

"But . . . but I thought she was moving home?" Myra spoke about her niece as though she were not at the table.

Emily picked up her wine glass and sighed. "I'm sitting right here."

Reaching under the table, Mark squeezed her knee. At least, Myra had been sidetracked from the best man topic.

"Have you taught them any mathematics?" Myra's question held a tone of indignation. She probably didn't expect an answer.

But Emily gave her one. "They can all count backward

from ten. Some of them can even count forward."

"Well!" Myra huffed. "As if that's education."

"Mostly we learned their names and how to read them and print them. And we talked about Christmas and what we would all do at Christmastime."

"And that's not going to bore you tomorrow?"

Emily thought about it. "Tomorrow, I think we'll make Christmas decorations." Turning to her sister, she said, "Remember when we used to make those ropes for the tree? With loops of green and red construction paper?"

"I remember that," Noelle said with enthusiasm. She sipped more wine.

"I love playing with scissors and glue." Emily warmed to the idea.

"Well, if it's only until Christmas, I suppose." Myra seemed satisfied with this possibility. And then she scowled, realizing she'd been derailed from her previous thought. She quickly found it again. "I want Dan to be—"

"I told Emily about the unicorn," Noelle said, tossing in another distraction.

Myra opened her mouth, as if about to speak and then closed it. She gave her head a slight shake, and then, "Oh yes," she said. "It's only fair, isn't it, Emily? Noelle will be the first to get married so she should have the unicorn."

Right, Mark thought. That made perfect sense.

"Unicorn?" Dan asked.

"It's a piece of crystal," Mark said, and right after he'd said it, he wished he'd kept his mouth shut. He didn't need to be in this conversation. He would simply enjoy the pizza.

"You've seen it?" Dan was surprised.

"Last night at Emily's apartment." *Wrong*. That had slipped out too.

"You were at Emily's apartment?" Dan and Myra spoke in unison.

"You mean that piece of glass you got from your old boyfriend?" Frank asked.

A momentary silence hit the table. Then Emily said, "Old boyfriend?"

And at almost the same time, Noelle said, "You had a boyfriend?"

"Of course I did," Myra answered, ruffling her feathers. "I had several suitors. But I chose to devote myself to my nieces."

"A boyfriend gave you the unicorn? I thought you bought it yourself." Emily seemed to be searching through memories.

"Yeah," Noelle said. "That time you were in Niagara Falls."

Another beat of complete silence. And then they heard Makita woof at the front door. With her special dog hearing, she'd probably heard another dog bark and, polite dog that she was, she was answering.

"Does the unicorn represent something?" Noelle stared at her aunt.

Emily concentrated on her wine glass, the golden liquid shining, the condensation beading on the outside. "He asked you to marry him." She stated it, as if it were an obvious fact. A fact she'd discovered right at this moment.

"Oh wow." Noelle's voice filled with awe. "And you said no." A tiny pause. "But you kept the unicorn."

"I don't want to talk about it," Myra said, flustered. "Emily will bring it home."

Never mind that Myra didn't want to talk about it, Noelle did. "But why—"

And then Myra did her own derailing. "I have the Swan Room booked."

This had the desired effect, because Noelle's mouth dropped open. "Aunt Myra! I told you I'm not getting married at your Country Club!"

"In case you change your mind. They said they'd hold it for me. For one more week."

"The Swan Room is quite lovely," Dan said, patting his napkin on his lips.

"Shut up," Noelle told him.

"I'm just saying your aunt has excellent taste."

Noelle glared at him. But Dan, the idiot, didn't get it. He kept talking. "I know Emily and I didn't manage to carry it off the first time, but that doesn't mean—"

"The *first* time?" Noelle's voice wavered.

Dan tightened his eyebrows and set his jaw. "There will be a second time," he stated. "Emily needs to mature a little and then—"

In a quick motion, Noelle picked up her slice of sausage and tomato pizza, and slapped it into Dan's face.

To his credit, he didn't jump away from the table, or move at all. As bits of sausage slid down his cheek and cheese plopped onto his perfectly ironed shirt, Noelle pushed away from the table, picked up her wine glass and left the room.

A second later, Emily stood, picked up her wine glass, and made a move to leave. Then she snatched the wine bottle from in front of Noelle's plate, and in another moment she was gone too, following her sister down the stairs.

In the quiet dining room, tomato sauce dripped off the end of Dan's nose. Frank stood up and pushed his chair back. "Would you like another beer?" he asked.

Chapter Nine

Myrrh is mine, its bitter perfume
breathes a life of gathering gloom

Sitting with Noelle on the couch downstairs, Emily looked out at the dark night. "I don't know why I thought she would be any different."

"She means well."

"She wants to choose the best man," Emily said. "How weird is that?"

Noelle focused on the rec room windows. "I won't let her." And then, more emphatically, "Troy won't let her." She sat up straight, perhaps gathering some strength. "Can you believe she booked the Swan Room?" A huge sigh. "That takes a special kind of insensitivity."

Sipping her wine, Emily heard the low murmur of voices filter down the stairs. "You mean, because that's where my rehearsal party was."

"No." Noelle's tone underscored her words. "Even if you hadn't had your rehearsal party there, I still would not want the Swan Room. I want something simple. Is there anything wrong with that?"

"Only that Aunt Myra seems to want the wedding she never had."

They were quiet a moment, thinking about Aunt Myra, and her boyfriend.

"It would not have worked," Noelle said.

"Hard to see Aunt Myra with a husband."

"He'd have to be pretty strong-willed."

"He'd have to be like Frank," Emily said, unable to picture her aunt and Frank together—an impossible image. But it was not impossible that Aunt Myra could ruin things for Noelle and Troy. "How does Troy feel about all her plans?"

"I told you. He wants to elope."

They heard the front door open, heard Makita woof, and the door closed again.

Was Frank leaving? Was Mark leaving with him? Emily tried to ignore her disappointment. It wasn't like she'd expected to talk to Mark tonight. But what had she expected?

Maybe a pleasant dinner? She'd have been better off with her candy canes and hot chocolate for dinner. Although . . . "That was funny. The pizza."

"Yes," Noelle said, perking up. "I enjoyed that."

"Aunt Myra will be upset."

"Of course she will."

"She means well."

"I know," Noelle said. "She *always* means well."

They both laughed.

In the backyard, a flicker of movement across the snow caught their attention. Frank's dog.

"That's Makita." Noelle stood and moved closer to the patio doors, watching as Mark carried a stack of wood to the fire pit. "He's building a fire!"

Hopeful, Emily felt a rush of warmth sweep through her. He hadn't gone. He hadn't left her. "Do we still have the old blankets?" she asked.

"In the chest by the door. The chairs are by the shed." Noelle headed for the stairs. "You stay here. I'll get the blankets. And our coats and boots."

A minute later, Noelle was tossing blankets down the

stairs. Emily collected them and stacked them. And then Noelle returned with their outdoor clothes.

Emily slipped on her Mukluks. "Is Dan still here?"

"Of course he is. He's ingratiating himself to Aunt Myra." Noelle zipped her coat. "And Frank's here too."

Maybe Frank would occupy Dan. Maybe Dan would not come outside. Maybe Dan would go away forever.

"Em?"

"Yes?"

"What happened that night?"

"It doesn't matter." Emily tugged on her mitts.

"You're never going to tell me?"

"Look. I accepted an ECS job today because of you. Don't ask any more than that."

Noelle grinned. "You didn't take the job because of me," she said, wrapping her scarf around her neck. "Admit it, you like those little kids."

Yes, she did like those little kids ... but they were messy and unorganized, and you never knew what was going to happen, or who might get hurt. "You get the blankets," she said. "I'll get the wine, and our glasses."

Carrying everything, they slipped out the patio doors and into the night.

It had stopped snowing. The sliver of a waning moon shed little light, and stars carpeted the sky, beaming in full brilliance. Heaps of snow covered the concrete cinder blocks surrounding the fire pit.

Emily dusted the snow off one of the blocks, and made a place for the wine and the two glasses. Mark knelt beside her, leaning into the fire pit, layering tiny bits of wood.

"Where did you get the kindling?"

"Dad always has kindling," he said. His dark hair fell forward, a few strands sifting over his eyes.

"Does Frank build fires here?"

"Are you kidding?" Noelle lugged the chairs to the patio. "You think Aunt Myra would let him build fires?"

Mark struck a match against a cinder block, creating a tiny flame that shivered in the darkness. "I'm surprised the fire ring is still here."

Emily handed him kindling and he coaxed the flame, building it slowly, letting the fire find its way. Mark had always been the best at building fires. Emily's fires had smoldered and gone out.

The chairs scraped on the patio as Noelle pushed them closer. "She wanted to get rid of it last summer," Noelle said, from somewhere behind them. "But I told her I might need it for a pre-wedding event."

The fire pit? "Not Aunt Myra's kind of event," Emily said.

"No, but she didn't want to take any chances with upsetting me. Not after you spoiled her summer solstice."

"I'm sure that was hard on her," Mark said, carefully adding more kindling.

And whether he meant leaving the fire pit, or spoiling summer solstice, he didn't sound like he cared.

The flames caught, licking along the dry wood, bursting a path of yellow and gold through the fire pit, sending a few sparks whirling up into the black sky. Then the growing fire threw its own light, masking the stars and the tiny moon.

Mark propped three logs across the new fire, high enough that they would not smother it, close enough that they would begin to burn. And then, satisfied the fire could take care of itself, he sat on the empty chair between Emily and Noelle, and Makita snuggled close to his feet.

The cold air frosted the wine glasses. Emily handed one to her sister and passed a blanket to Mark.

They'd done this before, many times. Sat around this fire pit and talked ... about difficult teachers, upcoming parties, the likelihood of passing exams, their heartthrobs and the best songs ever . . . and the latest nonsense Aunt Myra was putting them through.

They'd discussed and debated everything from favorite TV shows to how to fix the world . . . and solved nothing. It was an empty time, a catching up time, a slowing down the pace of life.

"This is nice," Emily said. "I've missed this."

"Me too." Mark reached for her glass, took a sip of the very chilled wine, and handed it back to her.

The same way he'd taken sips of wine from her glass when they'd toured through Las Vegas that night.

The yard was silent but for the crackle of the fire, the tiny hiss as the logs gently shifted in the growing flames.

"Is my dad still here?"

"Oh yeah," Noelle said. "He's complaining about the ceramic tile Aunt Myra used for the kitchen floor."

The renovation had been completed last month, but tonight was the first time Emily had seen it. She'd heard Aunt Myra talk about the renos on the phone, overjoyed to have the designer tile. "The tile," Emily said. "It's called premium something?"

"Premium Tuscany Gold Mosaic," Noelle answered. "Frank says it makes his feet cold."

"It is cold to walk on." Emily had felt the chill through her stockinged feet.

Mark settled the blanket across his knees "I notice Aunt Myra got him slippers."

"Yes." Noelle laughed. "But now he says if you drop a dish on the tile, it will break."

The fire sent a burst of sparks twirling up into the night.

"Does he drop a lot of dishes?" Emily asked.

"Of course not," Noelle answered. "But he needs something to complain about."

No one disagreed. They sat for several minutes, enjoying the winter silence, watching the flames, feeling the peace. And then Mark said, "Somebody should sneak in for more pizza."

"Can't," Noelle told him. "Dan's still here."

"Aunt Myra will insist on an apology," Emily said.

"No way." Noelle rearranged her blanket, snugging it around her knees. "I couldn't do that. Forget the pizza. We have wine."

Mark reached for Emily's glass, took another sip and returned it to her. Their gloved hands bumped against each other.

Noelle picked up the bottle and topped up her glass. "The great thing about a wine is that it clears your palette." She set the bottle down, clunking it on the cinder block, a loud sound in the quiet night.

Emily held her glass in front of her eyes, rotating the stem, watching the firelight bounce off the crystal. "The great thing about a wine," she said, "is that you get drunk."

Mark and Noelle laughed, and then Mark got to his feet, bunched up his blanket and dropped it in the chair. "I'm getting us some pizza." He headed inside, Makita following him.

"Dan had better not come out here." Noelle sighed. "And you had better not get drunk, Em. No telling what you'd say to him."

"Don't worry," Emily answered. "I won't get drunk."

Because she never did. She never drank enough to lose her natural caution. She was a careful person. She thought things out. She was not reckless.

Staring into the fire, she saw the reflection of the lights: the Las Vegas strip, the dancing fountains, the Luxor Sky Beam, the erupting volcano, the neon flamingos.

Three nights ago, she'd told herself she'd had too much wine. But that was not what had happened. She'd known what she was doing when she went to that Elvis Chapel and married Mark.

And it had nothing to do with too much wine.

Chapter Ten

All I want for Christmas

Perched on a stool behind the granite counter in Myra's sunny kitchen, Catherine stirred her tea and lemon. All she wanted was some Earl Grey, with milk, but Myra was insisting on this cinnamon stuff because it was Christmas.

Whatever. There was no point in discussing the tea, not when Myra was so upset about last night's pizza party.

"Why didn't Dan go outside and talk to her?" Catherine asked, still stirring her tea. "You finally get the two of them together and he doesn't make an effort?"

Myra sliced Christmas cake and set it on her Christmas china, the china with the holly sprig pattern.

"He said he wasn't dressed warmly enough." Myra arranged the little slices of cake. "I should have got rid of that fire pit a long time ago."

The fire pit was not the problem. "You can't blame the fire pit, Myra. And you can't blame Mark. Not this time."

"Then who can I blame?"

"You should have told Emily that you invited Dan."

"Don't be ridiculous. She would not have come. And anyway, it's Noelle's fault."

"Noelle?"

"For slapping pizza in Dan's face."

Catherine laughed. "Yes," she said, straightening, affecting a more somber tone. "Dan would not want another food fight with Noelle." She sipped the tea, doubted she'd ever develop a taste for it. "What did he say to upset Noelle so much?"

Myra thought a moment. "He said Emily was immature."

"He did?" Emily was anything but immature. Emily was rational and careful and old beyond her years. "Noelle sounds like the immature one. I mean, a food fight?" It was probably more than that. "Noelle must have been upset about something already."

Myra was silent. So, there *was* more to it. "What did *you* say to her?"

Myra sucked in air through her clenched teeth. "I told her Dan would be the best man."

"Troy's best man?" *Seriously?*

"Of course, Troy's best man. Who else is getting married?"

Catherine closed her eyes and sighed. "The groom picks his own best man."

"Not necessarily," Myra huffed. "Noelle should have a say in it."

"Hmmm. You may have a point." Usually, the groom would pick his own best man, but what if the bride objected? Thinking about her own fiancé, Catherine had an idea of Ryder's choice for a best man . . . and that was not anyone Catherine would choose.

"I want the Swan Room at the Country Club," Myra complained. "I don't know why Noelle has to be so stubborn."

"You do realize that place has bad memories for Noelle, since Emily ran out during her rehearsal dinner?"

"That was six months ago. And it was simply cold feet. If Emily could be back there again, why, she would feel more relaxed. All the attention would be on Noelle, and Emily wouldn't panic, and . . . " Myra brightened suddenly.

"It could even be a double wedding!"

Catherine choked on a cake crumb. "That might be overly optimistic."

"I know. I know. But fortunately, I'm good friends with the manager at the Country Club and the room is available on Christmas Eve. It can be set up with a day's notice and we still have two weeks to convince Noelle."

Good luck with that. With convincing Noelle. And, not only Noelle. "And, to convince Troy," Catherine added.

"Troy will do what Noelle tells him."

"You would think." But Catherine was learning that was easier said than done. For the most part, Ryder did what she told him. But sometimes he objected to the simplest things. Oh well, by the time they set a date for their wedding, she would have him trained.

"Well, do I?" Myra interrupted Catherine's musing.

"Pardon?"

"I don't need to be worried about Mark, do I?"

"Worried about what?"

"He seemed to be having a good time out there with Emily. They aren't . . . you know—"

"Are you kidding me? They're friends. Nothing more."

"Friends or not, he's a bad influence. That boy will never settle down." Myra shook her head and stared at the ceiling. "Although, when he wants to, he can be so charming."

"I suppose." Catherine conceded, though Mark was rarely charming around her.

"Nothing but compliments for my pizza," Myra said, beaming. "He took a whole tray of it out to the fire pit." She paused and tilted her head. "Why they want to eat out in the cold like that is beyond me." Dismissing Mark, Myra switched gears. "Did you know Emily has a job?"

"I know. She's at the library."

"A teaching job," Myra said, pouring her own tea.

Finally. "It's about time. She's lucky a position became available."

"Except—" Myra waited for Catherine's full attention— "it's at an elementary school."

"Elementary?" Catherine set down her cup. "Emily?"

"Kindergarten."

"No." *There must be some mistake.* "Are you sure?"

"Of course I'm sure."

"Emily cannot do kindergarten," Catherine said, pinching the edge of her saucer. "Kindergarten is random. Emily cannot do random."

Myra sighed. "I think her sister talked her into it."

Of course. Noelle did have a way of getting Emily to agree. "At least it's a teaching job, but—" Catherine noticed Myra's sad expression. "You don't seem happy about her getting the job."

"She would have moved back home," Myra said, with a tone of resignation. "She's easier to manage if she's living here. With her living on her own, I have practically no control over her."

Eeuw. "She is an adult, Myra. You're not supposed to control her."

"You know what I mean. She needs direction."

"Maybe, but—"

"I can't believe things are getting so complicated." Myra crossed the kitchen to where half a lemon dripped onto the cutting board. "I want Dan in the wedding party. With Emily. It will be the perfect chance for them to get back together." Myra sliced a wedge of the lemon. "And the bridal shower," she said, dropping the lemon into her tea. "I need to worry about Noelle's shower. Emily still hasn't done a thing about it." She took a quick sip of the tea, then added another thin slice of lemon. "And the weather." Myra frowned. "Oh dear."

Catherine turned to look out the window at the sun

shining and the snow dropping in clumps from the evergreen branches. "What about the weather?"

"The snow is melting. I want a white Christmas."

Catherine inhaled, long and deep. She admired the way Myra looked after her nieces, only wanting what was best for them. It was a mystery why Noelle was being so difficult, and Emily, too. Especially after everything their aunt had done for them. *Honestly.* Some people were just hard to understand. "We'll think of a way to get Dan in the wedding party. And you and I can plan the bridal shower. That should be easy enough." Catherine stared at the sliver of yellow rind floating in her tea. "But the weather? I don't know if we can manage the weather."

Gripping his full cup of coffee, Dr. Mark Bainbridge wove his way to a table in the corner of the hospital cafeteria where Pro sat reading something. Something glossy. A brochure.

Oh no. A brochure about cast care.

"What happened?" Mark asked as he reached the table.

Pro looked up, eyebrows lifted. "What do you mean?"

"Cast care?" Mark glanced at the brochure in Pro's hands. "Did your Aunt Tizzy have another fall?"

Pro stared at what he was holding and then carefully placed the brochure beside the napkin dispenser. "No. No," he said. "It was lying here. I just picked it up. She's fine."

Naturally, he picked it up. Pro read everything that crossed his line of vision.

Setting his coffee on the table, Mark collected his thoughts and then sank into a chair. Ten minutes ago, Pro had sent him a text, saying he was at the hospital and asking if they could meet, not saying why.

"I figured I was here—" Pro checked his cell, then set it

down. "—so I might as well touch base with you."

"About the . . ."

"Yes, about that."

About the divorce, and about what Mark had told Emily. Unfortunately, Mark had nothing to report, not yet. But . . . "Hasn't your Aunt Tizzy been discharged?"

"Yes. Yesterday morning."

"So you're here because?"

"She wanted me to bring cookies for the nurses on the ortho floor."

Of course she did. "Right."

"Sorry about worrying you," Pro said, still talking about his aunt. "She's fine, except it's hard to slow her down." Distracted, he paused, looked at his coffee and then grinned. "All I want for Christmas is to keep Aunt Tizzy off ladders."

They both laughed, but Mark wondered if something else had come up, about the divorce proceedings. And he hoped it was nothing that would upset Emily.

Anyway, there was no use rushing Pro when he was talking about his aunt.

"Did you help her with her tree?" Mark asked.

"I did. Last night," Pro told him, as he absently picked up the cast care brochure again, tapping it on the edge of his coffee cup. "This afternoon, her friends in the knitting club are coming over."

"Knitting?" An odd hobby for Pro's aunt. "Knitting doesn't seem like something that would interest her."

"She says she's always meant to learn. So she joined the knitting club and now she's on the board of directors."

"A knitting club has a board of directors?"

"Never mind. At any rate, I said I'd bring the cookies to the nurses and I thought I might as well check in with you. Have you talked to Emily?"

"Yes," Mark answered. "Well, no."

Pro waited.

Mark took a sip of his coffee, tasting the bitterness. Unfortunately, he was getting used to Kit's special blend and this was standard hospital issue. "I've seen her, twice since Monday," he said, "but I haven't been able to get her alone."

"Why not phone her?"

Because it wouldn't be right. "I thought this would be better in person."

Pro nodded, slowly, and looked at his coffee again.

"Believe me," Mark said. "All I want for Christmas is to get this Las Vegas paperwork sorted out."

Pro dropped the cast care brochure back on the table. "Just make sure she understands the timing," he said. "And get the marriage certificate as soon as—"

"I know," Mark said. "I'll call them on the fifteenth." He still needed to google the phone number so he was ready to call, but . . . "I only need to give them our names, right? They don't need to know anything else?"

"Like what?"

"Like the name of the chapel."

Pro frowned. "You don't remember the name of the chapel?"

Mark let out a long sigh. "There are a lot of chapels in Vegas."

"All right," Pro said. "But, you do know the name of the officiant?"

If only. "Elvis?"

Pro grinned, then his phone vibrated. Glancing at it, he said, "You'll figure it out." And then, "Ask Emily. She might have a better recollection."

She might, and maybe it didn't matter. Maybe all the paperwork would show up on schedule. And if for some reason it didn't, then he would start phoning chapels.

"Hey, Pro!" Kit approached the table.

"Dr. Livingston," Pro greeted their friend.

Kit sat quickly and turned to Mark. "I need to discuss that patient in 4A."

"That's next on the list," Mark told him.

"I'll let you guys get back to work." Pro picked up his phone, slipped it in his pocket and stood. "I'm behind, too."

"You're invited to the Christmas Eve wedding?" Kit asked as Pro moved away from the table.

"I am," Pro said. "You?"

"I'm covering for Mark," Kit answered. "Except, the way things are going, I'm not sure there will be a wedding."

Pro sat down again.

"I talked to Troy," Kit said. He turned to Mark. "Noelle's fiancé?"

"We've met." Mark had met Troy briefly, twice. The first time at Emily's rehearsal party—failed rehearsal party. And the next time in Vegas.

"I was out for a beer," Kit said. "With Troy and Ryder and Logan. Troy was telling us how he's having trouble dealing with Noelle's Aunt Myra."

Pro shook his head. "I'm not surprised."

"He's thinking of eloping."

Mark remembered Catherine saying the same thing, when they'd been on the plane. He hadn't taken her seriously. But, if Troy was actually thinking about eloping . . . well, that would not go over well with Myra.

"What about Noelle?" Pro asked. "What does she think?"

Kit shrugged. "She's thinking it might be a good idea."

"You can have Benjy's sandwich," Keith, the red twin, said.

The morning had flown by and lunch time had arrived.

Emily had been only slightly interrupted by thoughts of Mark, and last night, and the familiar fire in the fire pit.

Once again, they couldn't talk. And so, tonight she would phone him, and hope he answered and that he wasn't with anyone. Like Judith.

If he was, she'd ask him to call her back. She needed to find out what his lawyer friend, Pro, had said about the annulment.

A phone call would do. There was no use waiting until they could be alone together. They weren't meant to be together. In fact, it was not a good idea for them ever to be together—considering how she'd married him on the spur of the moment.

A scene from Saturday night flashed through her mind.

"Hey!" Mark called. "An Elvis Chapel!"

Sure enough there was one, right next to the bar they'd exited. In the next second, Mark had got down on one knee, right there in the street.

"Emily Marie Farrell, will you marry me?"

"Yes!" She'd answered without a moment of hesitation, and all around them the passersby on the street had cheered.

How had she ever thought she could marry Mark? Not commitment phobic Mark? And besides, they were *friends*, not lovers.

"Miss Emily? Are you hungry?"

"What?" The image of Las Vegas evaporated. "O-Oh, thank you, Keith. Thank you, Benjy. I'd love to have your sandwich."

That was true. Even though Emily had brought her lunch today—a container of cottage cheese—she much preferred the roast beef sandwich with the tangy Dijon mustard. And Benjy obviously preferred the peanut butter and raisin sandwich that Keith had given him.

The morning had started with *Anything Time*, as little

redheaded Francine called it. Groups of painters, block builders, rice table enthusiasts, readers, drawers and dreamers took up their stations throughout the room.

They met on the story mat about ten o'clock for a chapter of "Charlie's Christmas Eve Adventure", a story about a lost warthog trying to find his way home for Christmas. The chapter finished with Charlie's evil stepmother hiding his pencils so he couldn't write to Santa, and then they did a craft which involved counting out loops of construction paper and possibly some incidental learning of arithmetic.

Following that, there was more yoga—tree poses, airplane poses, cobras and breathing exercises.

For the whole morning, Benjy stayed under the teacher's desk.

The rest of the children focused on their activities, talked with each other, laughed and giggled, and tiptoed around Chewy the Gerbil, because they were still afraid he might die.

There must be some explanation for the children's fixation with death, but so far, Emily had not been able to figure it out. Probably something to do with television.

When the electronic noon bell buzzed, everyone dropped what they were doing, headed for their cubbies and lunch boxes, and returned to their assigned seats at the tables.

Like yesterday, the twins took charge of getting Benjy his lunch.

After lunch, same as yesterday, there was a rush to get outside and play in the snow. The children donned coats, hats, mitts and boots. The twins looked after getting Benjy dressed and promised him he could play in the igloo. Emily wasn't quite sure what the students did outside, but she didn't need to worry about them. For the next fifty minutes, the schoolyard supervisors took over.

All at once, the classroom was quiet. And then, Mr. Valentine opened the door and popped his head inside. He still wore the Santa hat. "I'll take them for a singalong this afternoon at two o'clock," he said, and he started to leave.

"Mr. Valentine?"

"Call me Howie." He waited, one hand on the doorknob.

Emily pulled open the top drawer of the teacher's desk and found the coil bound notebook with all its hurried entries. "I need to talk you about the notes the previous teacher left."

Surprise filled Mr. Valentine's features. "Mrs. Tadabousky left notes?"

Flipping to the page in question, Emily said, "I don't think so. I think Mrs. Jannie made these notes."

"Oh," he said. "Well, that makes sense." Then he quickly added, "Ivy will go over the notes with you."

"Ivy?"

"The school secretary. The old lady in the office. I know she acts like she has a screw loose but don't let her fool you. Nothing gets by her."

"So she's Mrs.—?"

"Mistle. Mrs. Mistle. It's a mouthful." He pulled back out of the room, letting the door close. "Just call her Ivy," he said, over his shoulder, and he was gone again.

Emily looked at the page in the notebook she was holding. Mrs. Jannie had written the word *family*—followed by a question mark—next to Benjy's name. But there was no clue to why the little boy was hiding under the desk.

Feeling herself slump, Emily closed the notebook. Soon enough, the mystery would be solved. For now, she needed a break. She'd go to the staffroom, eat Benjy's roast beef sandwich and get some coffee. But first, she'd check her cell.

Swiping the screen, she saw two messages.

One from Aunt Myra.

Call me. We need to discuss Noelle's shower.

Another from Catherine.

I have decided on a pattern for Noelle's china.

Of course Catherine would do that. Sometimes she had about as much tact as Aunt Myra. At any rate, Noelle would not go along with the china idea, even if she picked the pattern herself.

Emily sighed and put away her phone.

So, might as well admit it, she'd been hoping for a message from Mark. But there was nothing from Mark.

Chapter Eleven

Let nothing you dismay

Emily found her sister in a corner of the staffroom and sat beside her. "Catherine wants to do a china shower for you and she's picked out your pattern."

Noelle sputtered into her coffee. "She what?!"

"She picked—"

"She picked out a pattern! For me? Is she crazy? Nobody does that!"

Noelle rummaged in her poinsettia bag and found her cell. Emily leaned over and watched her sister type a quick text.

Shower canceled.

"Do you really think it will be that easy?" Emily asked.

"It should be." Noelle dropped the phone back in her bag. "Em, I'm ready to elope." She set her jaw then paused. "Only problem is . . ."

The problem was Aunt Myra, and her expectations. They had both given in to Aunt Myra for so long. To finally do what they wanted to do, that would be a drastic change.

"I can't back out, not after you canceled your wedding. I don't think Aunt Myra could handle two canceled weddings in one year."

Emily put her arm around her sister and thought about that. Maybe Aunt Myra could handle a lot more than they gave her credit for. "Never mind Aunt Myra," she said. "What do *you* want?"

Noelle let out a long, sad sigh. "At this point, I'm not sure."

"You love Troy?"

"I do. More than anything. But you loved Dan, and you walked out on your wedding."

"No."

"No, what?"

"No, I didn't love Dan."

Her sister waited. They'd never talked about that night.

"Not cold feet? Catherine and Aunt Myra keep saying it was cold feet."

"No, not cold feet." More like cold realization.

"Hmmm, okay." Noelle nodded.

"And . . ."

"And?"

"I think I may have wanted to get married, simply because I wanted to get away from Aunt Myra. Is that crazy?"

"Yes, it is," Noelle said. "But it still makes sense."

The staffroom buzzed with Christmas conversations— a mix of stress about finishing up classes and relief that the holidays would soon arrive. No one paid any attention to Emily and her sister as they quietly talked.

"I know the preparations are a hassle, but your wedding will be at home," Emily said. "There will be no practicing where to stand, no long walk down the aisle, and no need for pre-wedding jitters. It will be simple and calm. And perfect. A perfect Christmas Eve wedding."

"I don't know, Em. I have a bad feeling about this."

Weddings should not be so stressful. "Is it Aunt Myra? Or are you just not ready?"

"I don't know." Noelle stared at her feet, thinking. And then, "Em? What if Troy and I were to postpone? What if we waited for *you* to get married? You'll get married. Someday. Right?"

She already *was* married, and about to end the marriage.

"And then," Noelle said, brightening, "you can have the unicorn!"

At two o'clock, right after nap time, Mr. Valentine came into the classroom, wearing his Santa hat and carrying a guitar. He asked the children to line up in a row and, surprisingly, they followed the instruction. "We'll be in the music room for an hour," he told Emily. "That will give Ivy time to review things with you."

"You mean *Miss* Ivy, don't you Mr. Valentine?" Francine corrected him.

"Call me How—" He did a double take. "Yes, Francine, that is what I meant."

Turning to Emily, he said, "*Miss* Ivy should be here any minute."

Of course, he meant *Mrs.* Ivy, or rather, Mrs. Mistle, but at any rate, Emily was impressed with how he dealt with the children. And she found herself impressed, too, by the fact that although he was the principal, he made time for a singing class with the children.

And he played guitar. And built igloos. At her old job, the high school teachers were good at what they did, but they tended to specialize. Maybe a certain versatility was needed in elementary school. Maybe *she* could be more versatile.

In the quiet that followed, Emily fed the gerbil, cleaned up the rice table and organized the afternoon craft. Then she pulled her purse out of the cubby, found her phone and left a message for Mark.

Please phone me tonight.

Simple enough. No need to meet in person. And soon she would know what had to be done to get this paperwork over with before Aunt Myra had any idea a marriage had ever taken place.

In the meantime, Benjy stayed under the desk. He seemed happy enough there, reading a picture book and holding on tight to his teddy bear.

Emily checked the time and wished the secretary, Mrs. Ivy Mistle, would show up, but the woman was not punctual. At least, not today.

While Emily waited, she reviewed the scribbles in Mrs. Jannie's notebook, getting lost in the little comments.

> *Ryan demonstrates ++ creativity at the craft table.*
>
> *Kyle excels at Phys Ed.*
>
> *Tina and Billy work well together.*

Finally, at five minutes to three, the door swung open. The old secretary staggered into the classroom, and immediately fumbled a stack of green folded papers in a fan around her feet.

"Whoops." She bent and started gathering the papers.

Emily set a new stack of pictures books on the floor, within Benjy's reach, and rushed over to help Mrs. Mistle.

"Christmas concert programs," Mrs. Mistle said.

"Christmas concert?!" *What Christmas concert? Nobody had said anything about a Christmas concert!*

"Didn't you know? We have a concert on the twenty-second, the last day of school, beginning about two o'clock. Mrs. Jannie was planning something." Mrs. Mistle stood, tapping the programs back into a neat pile. "I don't know what it was, but it's probably in her book."

"A Christmas concert." That was the last thing Emily needed. Herding twenty-four little children into some kind of presentation ... assuming she could get Benjy to participate, and that was unlikely. In fact, it was unlikely Emily could come up with anything worth performing. She did not have the skills to do a Christmas concert presentation.

"I'm supposed to go over the student concerns with you," Mrs. Mistle said.

Emily brought her focus back to this meeting. She'd worry about the concert later, and hopefully she would find a way to get out of it.

"Let's see. First of all." Mrs. Mistle held up one hand, counting off on her fingers. "Don't let the twins trick you. One is supposed to be red and one is supposed to be blue. But sometimes they change clothes so you can't tell them apart."

"They're fraternal," Emily said, automatically, unable to quit thinking about the possibility of having to do a Christmas concert.

"They look identical to me." Mrs. Mistle shrugged.

"Not quite identical." Emily didn't have trouble telling them apart, although she *had* noticed they'd changed sweaters yesterday afternoon.

"Whatever." Mrs. Mistle held up a second finger. "Don't let Francine boss you around." A third finger. "Kyle eats playdough. Best to keep him away from it." Then she held up a fourth finger, stared at it and frowned. "What else? There was something else."

Emily assumed Mrs. Mistle would say something about Benjy under the desk, so she pointed down.

"What?" Mrs. Mistle looked confused. And then, suddenly understanding, she said, "Oh yes. Is he still there?" She bent, took a quick look, and Benjy scurried deeper under the desk. "I heard about Mrs. Tadabousky trying to drag him out," the secretary said. She shook her head. "That didn't go over well. Of course you must know—"

A loud commotion out in the hallway interrupted them. It sounded like a chorus of singers tuning up, all in different keys. With a loud bang, the door burst open and Mr. Valentine led the troop of ECS students into the classroom. They were singing "The Wheels on the Bus" and making windshield wiper motions with their hands as they marched.

Mrs. Mistle smiled at the children as they filed into the room. And then, above the noise, she said, "Now where was I? I told you about the twins?"

"Yes, you did."

"And make sure you close the gerbil's door." Mrs. Mistle squinted, thinking hard. "Oh! And you must visit your sister's classroom. She has a little lamb in there."

"A little lamb?"

"A real lamb, with straw and everything. The desks are in a circle and the lamb wanders around inside the circle."

Noelle had not mentioned this.

Emily's phone was still on top of the teacher's desk. It beeped a message notification. Unable to resist, she picked up the phone, checked the message readout. It was from Mark.

I'll bring dinner tonight.

On his way to Emily's apartment, Mark picked up a barbecued chicken from Notables, along with the usual seasonal vegetables. Right now, that meant parsnip, broccoli and butternut squash. He also picked up a couple servings of the fingerling potatoes and the artisan green salad. Enough food for four people, which was a good thing, because she'd have leftovers for tomorrow night. She needed to eat more than cottage cheese.

And, she wasn't going to like the timing for the divorce.

A year was a long time—she wanted the divorce now. He'd give her the news and then they'd eat. Hopefully the food would help to cheer her up.

As he stepped through the puddles of melting snow, he suddenly remembered the chapel package. The big cardboard box had arrived today—it was sitting on his kitchen table and he hadn't remembered to bring it. At least, he had her camera with him. It was still in his coat pocket from last time.

They could talk about the divorce first. Get that out of the way. Then they'd eat. Then they could laugh about the pictures they'd taken that night.

Juggling the bags of food, he buzzed her unit.

"Hello?" someone answered. Not Emily. *Noelle?* Was she here again? Had she moved out of Myra's house too?

"It's Mark."

"Come on up!"

It *was* Noelle and she sounded happy—at least, she sounded like her usual self. Last night, at pizza night, Noelle had been upset with her aunt. And no wonder, with Myra trying to choose the best man, trying to choose the location for the wedding, and generally trying to run all over Noelle's wishes. Typical Myra.

When the elevator doors opened on the seventh floor, Noelle was standing in front of them.

"You brought food! I love you!" she said, taking one of the bags. "I was going to suggest we go out to eat and here you are." She looked more closely at the bags. "Notables! My absolute favorite." She led the way to Emily's apartment.

As Noelle carried the food to the kitchen. Emily came out of her bedroom and gave him a shrug. Obviously, with Noelle's impromptu visit, they would not be discussing the divorce. And, good thing he hadn't brought the chapel package. That would have been hard to explain.

Noelle opened the fridge and took out a bottle of white wine, probably her traditional Chardonnay. "Guess what? Emily has to do a Christmas concert."

"I think I can get out of it," Emily said as she set plates on the counter. "I am a substitute, after all."

"Substitute, nothing." Noelle turned to him. "Do you want some wine, Mark? Of course you do." She headed for the cupboard that had the tumblers. And then, speaking to her sister again, she said, "It's your fear of the unknown."

"I don't have a fear of the unknown."

"A fear of the unknown. A fear of flying. It's all related."

"I don't have a fear of flying. I have a fear of crashing."

A bouquet of red roses sat on the counter in the kitchen.

"They're from Dan," Noelle told him. "That guy never gives up."

"Dan was here?"

"No. Well, yes. He left the flowers by Emily's door, and Mrs. Harcourt isn't home." A little pause. "Normally, Emily gives the flowers to Mrs. Harcourt."

"Of course she does," Mark said, as he hung his coat in the closet—leaving Emily's camera in his pocket.

"So since Mrs. Harcourt isn't home, Emily was going to throw the roses in the garbage. But I'm taking them home."

He approached the counter, and the roses. "They're . . . nice," he said.

Noelle handed him the red tablecloth. "For Emily's *table*," she said, meaning the overturned packing crate in the living room. "Take the candles too." She passed him the red pillar candles they'd used on Monday night.

He set the candles on the carpet and fanned the tablecloth over the crate. The two cushions and the yoga bolster were still arranged around the *table*.

"Do you think he'll ever give up?"

"Give up?"

"Wanting to marry my sister."

"He does seem determined."

With the bottle of wine tucked under her arm, Noelle brought the plates and cutlery and three tumblers to the table. Emily brought the two bags of food, handed one to him and they started unpacking the carryout while Noelle arranged the dishes.

"Would you?" Noelle asked him.

"Would I what?"

"Give up? If you had a chance to marry my sister, would you give up?"

"I'd marry her in a heartbeat." And he had, four nights ago. Now he was divorcing her. Why was he doing that?

Because—a little voice told him—they were friends and he wanted them to keep being friends. Marriage didn't work.

Noelle laughed. "Like you'd ever get married." She started pouring the wine. "Are you still going out with Judith?"

"That's not serious."

"But are you still going out with her?"

"I think so."

Noelle handed him a tumbler of wine. "No wonder Aunt Myra is worried about you."

"She is?"

"She's been worried about you practically since she started taking care of us."

"That's because she's never been able to control me, like she controls you two."

"She doesn't control us," Noelle insisted.

"She does her best," Mark answered.

"She means well," Noelle said. "So we try to go along with what she wants and not hurt her feelings."

Emily and Noelle tiptoed around Myra, as if they were afraid of losing their substitute parent. At some point, they'd figure out that Myra didn't need any propping up.

And, at some point, he'd have to deal with Judith. It was Wednesday now and he'd been home since Sunday night and he still hadn't phoned her. She'd been sending him texts. Mostly cute little things. But last night she'd asked if he was sick, as if that were the only reason he wouldn't get back to her.

He would get back to her, as soon as he figured out what to say. It was confusing.

"Let's drink a toast," Noelle said, holding up her tumbler of wine.

"To?" Mark held up his glass.

"To us," Noelle said. "It's the third time this week that we're all together."

"It does feel good to be back together," Mark said.

"Yes, it does." Emily raised her tumbler, and they all clicked glasses.

He continued holding his tumbler up, stared at it. "Open the wedding gift from me," he told Emily. "The wine glasses are not for your Dan wedding. Pretend they're for a much nicer wedding."

Thinking of their Las Vegas wedding, he sent her a sly smile. She closed her eyes and gave her head a little shake.

"Seriously, I want you to have the wine glasses."

"They're quite elegant," Noelle said.

Emily frowned. "How would you know?"

"I helped pick them out. He wanted to make sure he got you something you'd like."

A little smile played across Emily's face. "Thank you," she said. "I'll pick up the wine glasses when I bring the unicorn over." And then, turning to her sister, "Or, better yet— Why don't you bring the unicorn home tonight?"

"No. With my luck I'll drop it and Aunt Myra would never forgive me," Noelle said. "You bring it next time you come over."

"Last time, didn't work so well."

"I don't think she'll surprise you with Dan again."

Emily breathed out a long sigh. "I'm not so sure about that."

They opened the cartons and loaded their plates.

Noelle sipped her wine, considered it, and drank a bit more. "You have no sense of commitment, Mark."

"I don't?"

"Probably because your mother divorced your father."

What? "That has nothing to do with anything."

"You always said it didn't bother you, when your mother left."

"It didn't." And why was Noelle talking about his mother and the divorce?

"You were only ten years old."

"Nine," he said, without thinking.

"It probably bothered you," Noelle went on. "You're in denial, that's all."

He wasn't in denial. He was completely over that part of his life. "The thing about people on the verge of marriage," he said, "is they think everyone else should get married too."

"But don't worry." Noelle ignored his comment. "I bet that if you ever *do* get married, you'll never get divorced."

"Nine years old," Emily muttered, lost in some long ago memory.

"Yeah, nine years old," Noelle repeated. "And Emily was nine when our parents were in that accident."

Emily touched her sister's shoulder. "You were only seven," she said, a wistfulness in her voice.

"I think it was harder on you than me, when they died." Noelle swirled her wine in the tumbler. "I had you to look out for me. You didn't have anyone."

"She had me," Mark said, wondering how much Noelle had already had to drink.

"Yes, but you're not the type to stay."

"Okay!" Emily held up her hands, as if she were hushing her kindergarten class. "That's enough gloomy reminiscing for one night. Let's eat."

Yes, enough gloomy reminiscing, Mark thought, and he was happy when the conversation shifted to what Emily could do with her class for the Christmas concert. At least, Noelle kept coming up with ideas and Emily kept coming up with excuses for not participating.

Finally Noelle gave up and quit talking about the concert. But then she turned her attention to him. "You should marry Emily," she said. "That would really piss off Aunt Myra." She laughed. "Could you imagine? Emily and Mark. That's funny."

"Yes, very funny," Mark said, trying not to look guilty, and trying not to look at Emily.

"You know who should *not* get married?" Noelle asked.

"You're going to tell us," Emily said.

Noelle looked at him, raised her eyebrows.

He nodded. "Sure," he said. "Tell us."

"Catherine and Ryder." Noelle topped up her wine. "I mean, I like Catherine. But I just don't see it working out with Ryder."

As a matter of fact, he didn't see it working either. But that was for Ryder to figure out.

Emily didn't comment on the Catherine-Ryder match, but she suddenly held up a hand. "I've figured out your shower," she said, looking pleased with herself. "We'll do it on Saturday."

"This Saturday?"

"Yes."

"But not china," Noelle said. "Definitely not china."

"No, we'll do what we were doing in kindergarten today."

Noelle waited.

"We'll make Christmas ornaments. Sparkly angels."

Noelle brightened, obviously liking this idea.

"I have tons of supplies from Mrs. Jannie," Emily said. "Little wooden heads."

"With smiles?"

"Of course with smiles. And different colored wings—those foil wings with the designs? In blue and green and gold—and gold and silver pipe cleaners for the halos. And sparkly string for hangers. And these tiny little tags for people to write their names and good wishes for you and Troy."

"I'll have a whole tree of angels!"

"We'll put them all in one of those big Christmas boxes," Emily went on. "Aunt Myra can bake. That should keep her happy. We'll supply the coffee and tea. And we'll have it in the school gym."

"Perfect," Noelle said. And then, "Do you want to come, Mark?"

"To make Christmas angels? Are you kidding?"

"You're a surgeon." Noelle shrugged. "You should be able to handle a little cutting and sewing."

Chapter Twelve

The stars are brightly shining

The next morning Emily walked to Winward Elementary, ready to start her third day of teaching ECS.

She could see the new moon, low in the eastern sky, struggling to shine between the everchanging winter clouds. Behind her, a Chinook arch spanned the western sky, announcing the dry winds that would suck up the snow, and leave the roads and yards a bare winter gray. Mother Nature didn't seem to care a bit about Aunt Myra's plans for a white Christmas.

And fate didn't seem to care a bit about Emily and her need to know the status of her annulment.

Thursday already, she and Mark still had not been able to talk. Although, she had to admit, last night had been a lot of fun. Almost like the old days, when they'd been constant friends.

And now those days were gone. They were still friends, but not *constant* friends like when they'd lived next door to each other. Even then, it had been so hard seeing him go out with all those different girls . . . and knowing *she* would never go out with him. Not if she wanted to keep him for a friend. To keep him always. To not become just another girl in a long string of fleeting relationships.

Taking a big breath of the chilly air, Emily lifted her

head and promised herself there would be better days ahead. In fact, even now, things were better. For one, she had this teaching job. It was ECS, but it was still a teaching job. It would pay the bills and, surprisingly, she found she was enjoying her time with the children.

No mistakes could be made in ECS. The students would learn whatever they would learn and it didn't matter. There were no university admission tests to deal with. Nothing for Emily to worry about.

Today, during her breaks, she would check with Mrs. Mistle in the office and make sure she could rent the gym for Noelle's bridal shower on Saturday.

She would text Mark and arrange a time when they could talk on the phone.

And she would find Mr. Valentine and tell him there was no way she could prepare her class for a Christmas concert.

At noon, Emily met her sister in the staffroom for lunch.

"You seem to be liking Benjy's roast beef sandwiches," Noelle said.

Emily looked at the waxed paper wrapped sandwich in her hand. "He gave it to me first thing this morning, before he crawled under my desk."

"Hey!" one of the teachers called from across the room. "I hear there's a party on Saturday."

"Sure is," Noelle answered. "You're all invited to my shower. One o'clock. Bring your creativity."

The gym was booked from one o'clock until five—and at no cost. "You're our teachers," Mrs. Mistle had said, clasping her hands, palm to palm. "This is a staff social!"

Everyone liked the idea of making a Christmas ornament. And everyone looked forward to homemade baking, tea and coffee, and a time to get together as adults only.

"No fear of flying?" Noelle asked her.

"What?"

"I think ECS is good for you." Noelle was in a philosophical mood. "You don't have the same worries you did in high school. So, no fear of flying."

"It's not related," Emily insisted. "But maybe I don't have the fear of making mistakes like I had with my high school students. Nothing is crucial in ECS."

"You see? You're learning something new!"

"But I don't want to do a Christmas concert. I hate performances."

"Don't think of it as performing."

"It *is* performing."

"No, it's the kids having a good time. It's not supposed to be perfect. It's supposed to be fun."

At any rate, Emily was unable to track down Mr. Valentine and bail on the concert. He was always busy somewhere—teaching the grade fours ukulele or teaching cursive writing to the grade threes or doing singalongs with the other grades.

Not only that, she was unable to get in touch with Mark, although he'd sent one text.

On call. Talk soon.

Sometimes when he was on call, he had stretches of time when no one needed him at the hospital. Maybe he would phone later tonight . . .

On Friday, much the same thing happened. Mr. Valentine remained unavailable. All the teachers were busy with concert preparations. But kindergarten had its own pace and a kind of calmness.

Morning flowed from an hour of Free Play—what Francine called Anything Time—to story time, to craft time, to yoga, to lunch. After lunch, the children took their blankets from their cubbies and sat on the story mat. There was another chapter of "Charlie's Christmas Eve Adventure" in which Charlie helped the other little warthogs escape from the cellar where they'd been trapped by the evil stepmother.

Then the children curled up with their blankets and nodded off to sleep for about forty-five minutes. When they woke up, they wanted to sing Jingle Bells, with hand motions for ringing the bells, the way Mr. Valentine had taught them during Wednesday's singing class. So they did.

Then, for something different, Emily took her students for a visit to Noelle's classroom—to see the little lamb.

Even Benjy came with them. But as soon as they returned to their own classroom, he disappeared back under the teacher's desk.

Then, there was a craft time.

The children made loops of construction paper into garlands—which involved some counting. They could all count *forward* to ten now, as well as backward.

Throughout the day, the twins took care of Benjy. The children tiptoed around Chewy. And there were three texts from Mark as he moved from crisis to crisis at the hospital.

Skiing accident.

Roof and Christmas lights.

I'll get back to you.

That was all. He was either very busy at the hospital, or he was avoiding her.

. . . . .

Saturday afternoon arrived with warm Chinook winds bringing the temperatures above freezing.

At the school, the caretaker had arranged tables in the gym for Noelle's shower. Several of the teachers helped by bringing in tablecloths and setting the tables with wedding-themed napkins and confetti. The old secretary, Mrs. Mistle, was in charge of the tea and coffee.

The grade two teacher filled a table with the ornament supplies: wooden angel faces, sheets of craft foil for the angel wings, glittery string, pipe cleaners for the halos, tags, and scissors with rounded tips. There was also a large shiny box patterned with little reindeer. Stacks of green and red tissue paper were arranged next to the box.

At about a quarter to one, Aunt Myra and Frank carried in trays of her baking. Emily recognized almond snowballs, peppermint pinwheel cookies, buttercream cookies, and oh my, her favorite gooey chocolate drop cookies. There were also pumpkin spice cookies with crushed candy cane topping, fruit cake cookies and several other kinds of squares and cookies she'd never had before. The grade four teacher helped with arranging the trays on a long table at the front of the gym. And then the party started.

Everyone made a Christmas angel, including Frank. They added a tag with their name and a wish for the happy couple. Then each angel was carefully wrapped in tissue paper and placed in the shiny box.

Because there were a lot of decisions involving the color of wings and halos, the project took about an hour. By two o'clock, Mrs. Mistle had the tea and coffee ready and everyone loaded their plates with homemade goodies.

Aunt Myra got so many compliments on her baking that she seemed to forget the shower was held in a lowly gymnasium.

Even Frank complimented her baking. Referring to a

coconut chocolate concoction, he said, "These are *remarkably* good." And then he added, "Which is why I'm mentioning it."

"Pardon?" Aunt Myra asked.

"If they're good," he said, "you remark on it. So I did. These are *remarkable*."

Unsure of whether she'd been complimented, or joked with, Aunt Myra frowned. Then, apparently deciding that it was a compliment, she smiled at Frank and offered him another cookie.

Catherine joined Emily and Noelle near the coffee urn. "You really should have your reception at the Country Club," she told Noelle.

"I want to get married by the fireplace," Noelle said, without hesitation, since she was practically immune to these suggestions by now.

Not listening to Noelle and still talking about the Country Club, Catherine carried on. "It's such a beautiful venue," she said, with a dreamy look in her eyes.

"Plus," Noelle added, as she picked up a peppermint pinwheel, "there's no way Troy would agree to the Country Club."

Catherine tilted her head, looking thoughtful. "You have to work on him."

"Work on him?" Noelle took a bite of the cookie. "What are you talking about?"

"You can't expect him to be perfect right off the bat," Catherine said, as if she were discussing a recipe. "I mean, Ryder's not perfect. But once we're married, I'll fix him."

"You'll *fix* him?"

"You know what I mean," Catherine said. She sipped her tea. "He has a few rough edges that need smoothing. Of course, I love him but I'll be able to love him more."

Noelle rolled her eyes and Emily tried not to laugh as she watched the two of them talk.

"Now Dan," Catherine said, "I don't think he needs fixing."

"No, you wouldn't," Noelle said.

"He's funny." Catherine held up one finger. "He has a lot of friends." Another finger, as she made a list, counting it off. "He dances so well. And, wow, that proposal."

Catherine was referring to Dan's New Year's Eve proposal during the dinner at the posh Chez Jubenville.

"That was *so* romantic." Catherine closed her eyes a moment, savoring the memory. When she opened her eyes again, she saw another one of their friends, excused herself and wandered off to visit.

Watching Catherine leave, Noelle said, "Aunt Myra did quite a job with it, didn't she?"

"With?"

"With your proposal party."

Last New Year's Eve, Aunt Myra had arranged the huge dinner party with the attentive waiters, the romantic background music, the elegant table settings and the beautiful candelabras.

"It should have been romantic," Emily said, "but it seemed like . . . I don't know."

"Like he was proposing to Aunt Myra?"

Emily turned to her sister, surprised that she would say that.

"Well," Noelle added with a shrug, "Aunt Myra is the one who said yes."

That was true. Aunt Myra had been the one to start jumping up and down before Emily had a chance to say anything.

In fact, Emily never had said yes. She'd just kind of nodded while Dan slipped the ring on her finger, pulled her into his arms and kissed her, in front of the crowd of guests. And then the waiters had started passing around champagne.

"I wasn't sure what it would feel like ... getting proposed to ... but I somehow didn't think it would feel like that," Emily told her sister. "Like it was ... I don't know."

"Orchestrated?"

"Yes, orchestrated." Like all the things Aunt Myra did so perfectly.

Mrs. Mistle tottered across the room, balancing a tray of Aunt Myra's pumpkin spice cookies. She came to stop beside them, next to the coffee urn. "You did well getting so many volunteers to set this up on short notice," she told Emily.

"Yes, I did." Emily eyed the cookies, thinking about having another one. The crushed candy cane topping sparkled in the gym's overhead lights.

"Everyone loves a party," Noelle said. "And this was a great idea. The Christmas angels are beautiful."

Emily hugged her sister. "I wish I could get some classroom volunteers for myself. The ECS mothers are all so busy this time of year."

"I know," Noelle agreed. "All the parents are busy right now."

They stood together near the stage and listened to Mrs. Mistle go on about the Christmas concert preparations. And then the old lady jerked her head up. "I just remembered! Oh, I'd better go tell the caretaker." And off she hurried with her tray of cookies and her wobbly gait.

Watching the secretary cross the gym, Emily had a sudden idea. "Maybe I could ask Aunt Myra?"

"Ask her what?"

"To be a volunteer."

"In ECS? Are you sure that's a good idea?"

"Why not? It's not the sort of thing where she could do any interfering."

"Hmmm."

"And she was good about today," Emily rationalized. "Plus, I bet she'd enjoy herself. It would give her a sense of purpose."

Noelle laughed. "I don't think you or I will ever get over this need to take care of her."

"She means well," Emily said. "And since you're not going along with her Country Club plans, volunteering here might bolster her ego."

"Hmmm." Noelle was still not convinced.

"She could make gingerbread men and the students could decorate them."

"Hmmm." Noelle thought about it some more. And then, "As long as she doesn't insist on those little kids doing it her way."

"I don't think they'd listen," Emily said.

At four o'clock, Mark signed off on his last case. Dr. Kit Livingston had arrived in the ER a few minutes ago, looking rested and ready to take over. Mark briefed him on the outstanding concerns.

"Got any plans tonight?" Kit asked.

"Go home and have a nice long shower," Mark said. He also planned on seeing Emily, although he didn't mention that.

The ER doors swooshed open as he exited the hospital. It was almost dark, and only half past four. As the winter solstice approached, the days grew shorter.

Six months ago on the eve of the summer solstice, Emily had walked out on her wedding rehearsal party—and she still hadn't told him why. Not that there'd been many opportunities to talk about it, because they didn't spend much time together. At least, they usually didn't. However, since meeting her a week ago in front of Caesars, they'd been spending a lot of time together. And hopefully, they could spend some time together tonight. Alone.

Noelle would not interrupt them this time. Troy was taking her out after she finished with the bridal shower at the school. And Ryder had told him he was taking Catherine to some fancy restaurant she liked. Myra would never come to Emily's apartment. Dan might, but apparently he only dropped off flowers.

But, would Emily be at her apartment? What if she had other plans?

Pausing on the sidewalk, Mark retrieved his cell, checked the readout, and felt his jaw clench. Another text from Judith.

> *Miss you!*

That was all it said. Plus, a lot of smiley faces. He shook his head, letting go of the sudden guilt that had appeared out of nowhere. He'd get back to Judith, soon.

As soon as he figured out what to tell her. And, there was nothing to tell her, not really. It wasn't like he and Judith were in a serious relationship.

He found Emily's last text. It had been on Thursday, about noon, two days ago. She'd asked him to phone.

But he couldn't just phone. She was expecting a simple annulment, and now he had to tell her they needed a divorce and it would take over a year. That's not something you said on the phone. However, things had been so hectic at the hospital, he hadn't been able to phone.

Well, he admitted, he might have squeezed out five minutes, but he didn't want to phone. He wanted to see her. To be with her. It only seemed right, after all.

He texted—

> *Bringing chapel package.*
> *Got any food?*

He doubted it. Her Aunt Myra could have sent more

cinnamon buns. And maybe there were leftovers from today's bridal shower. But those were all sweet things, nothing substantial. He'd go home and have a shower, pick up the chapel package and her camera, and they could go out to the Keg.

At half past five, Mark pulled into the Visitor Lot at Winward Groves. Before turning off the engine, he hit the windshield washer, clearing the spatters that threatened to obscure his vision. The Chinook had warmed the city, much of the snow had melted and the streets were muddy.

Windshield clear, he checked his phone again. Still no message from Emily. Just his luck.

Disappointed, he dropped his head on the steering wheel. What should he do?

He could buzz her unit. Maybe she wasn't checking her phone? That was it. That was a reasonable explanation.

As he got out of his SUV, he had a fleeting thought. He'd never worried about getting in touch with her before. She was always there, whenever he needed her.

A few minutes later, with the chapel package tucked under his arm, he buzzed her unit. And waited, and then buzzed again.

"Go away!"

Interesting. She sounded angry. Dan must have been here. Now what?

Just then, an old gentleman with a bushy gray beard and a red toque, pushed open the door and held it for Mark. Mark thanked the man, went inside, and wondered about the building's security.

When he got off the elevator on the seventh floor, he found Emily in the hallway outside the apartment closest to the elevator.

She was talking to an old lady whose hair was fluffy

white and streaked with pink highlights. The woman wore a long cotton dress, a gypsy style, with a multitude of colors in patchwork designs. Some of the patches were orange and brown floral patterns, some were stripes of blue, orange, purple and yellow. The dress came to just above her ankles. Her feet sported low black leather sandals and her toenails were painted bright red.

When Emily saw him, she smiled. "Mark!"

Good. She was glad to see him. Today she was in a green silk blouse, open at the collar, and dark green pants. More dressy than usual, but she was coming from the bridal shower. She'd traded her shoes for the big gray socks she liked to wear around her apartment.

As he approached, she said, "Mrs. Harcourt, this is my friend, Mark. Mark, Mrs. Harcourt."

"How do you do?" Mrs. Harcourt beamed up at him. "I hope you like mac and cheese." She held a round red ceramic dish with a lid on top. Similar to the one they'd had on Monday night with the Irish stew. "This is full of cheese—three kinds—and sour cream too."

"Thank you so much," Emily said, accepting the dish.

"Thank you, dear, for the flowers. They're beautiful."

A phone started to ring from inside Mrs. Harcourt's apartment. "That will be my daughter," Mrs. Harcourt said. "See you later!" and she was gone.

The door swung closed with a decisive clonk.

Turning to Emily, he noticed how the green silk of her blouse accented the gold of her hair. When he realized he was staring, he shook his head, cleared his thoughts . . . brought his mind back to Mrs. Harcourt. "Interesting lady," he said.

"Yes," Emily agreed. "Interesting and wonderful. She feeds me."

"I'm glad." And then, because he needed to know, "More red roses?"

"Orange this time." Emily kicked aside her white Mukluks. They had been holding her apartment door open. "Mrs. Harcourt says that orange means new beginnings."

Really? "Does Dan know that?"

"I doubt it," she said. "Are you hungry?"

"I am." They were inside her apartment now. She set the casserole on the counter. "What's that package?"

"The chapel package."

"Oh." A shy smile.

"Lighten up," he said. "Is it so terrible being married to me?"

"No. It's not terrible at all. I just don't want Aunt Myra finding out."

"Let's not worry about Aunt Myra tonight."

Emily shrugged and looked up at him with those clear blue eyes.

He'd never noticed how blue her eyes were. It was the green silk, somehow making her eyes look bluer. He blinked. "And I have your camera."

"Oh." Another shy smile.

"I'll bet we got some great pictures." He laughed.

"That need to be deleted!"

"I thought you'd say that. But we're going to look at them first."

She grimaced. "Oh my God. I need wine."

He should have brought some. "Do you have any?"

"A whole case," she said. "Noelle gave it to me. Her favorite Chardonnay."

"And the wine glasses?" The ones he'd given her as gift for her almost wedding to Dan?

"Yes, she brought those over too. But she wouldn't take the unicorn. I have to bring that to Aunt Myra myself. Noelle is afraid she'll drop it, or otherwise damage it."

He set the chapel package on the counter beside the

casserole. And he put her camera there too. Only the kitchen light was on. Dark night showed beyond the living room windows.

"You didn't get my text?" he asked.

"No," she said. "I've been avoiding my phone. Did you get my text?"

"The Thursday one? Yes."

"You didn't need to come here. We could have talked on the phone."

"I didn't want to phone. I wanted to open the chapel package together. It'll be fun."

"Fun?" She closed her eyes and gave her head a slight shake. "Tell me what your lawyer friend said."

"All in good time. Let's eat first."

"Okay." She took out two plates. "Want to eat at the counter?"

"Where are the wine glasses?"

"Top of the fridge. I haven't opened the box yet. Noelle brought it over just before the shower."

"Let's eat in the living room," he said. "With the candles. You'll like these glasses. They look best by candlelight."

"A candlelit dinner of mac and cheese and Chardonnay." She tilted her head, thinking about that. "Sounds romantic."

"It *is* romantic."

His job was the tablecloth and candles. He fanned the red tablecloth over the packing crate and then set the red pillar candles in the center of it. Since he was near the windows, he looked down at the circular drive, seven floors below.

The snowman was still there, but with the Chinook, he had lost his head. A few stars peeked out between the blowing winter clouds. There was no moon that he could see.

Emily carried plates, cutlery, a bottle of wine and the corkscrew to the table. He brought the casserole, and then the package of wine glasses.

Her stereo was playing Christmas Celtic instrumentals. A new song started. A lilting adaptation of "It Came Upon A Midnight Clear".

"Yoga bolster for you?" she asked, lighting the candles.

"Yes," he said. "My usual spot." His spot for the third time this week.

She sat in her usual spot, on the cushion in front of the bookcase. The crystal unicorn stared down at them from the top shelf.

"I wrapped this." He handed her the package of wine glasses. "You can open it."

"Thank you," she said, with a smile so beautiful it was as if he'd given her the keys to a kingdom. Carefully she removed the shiny gold paper. Then she set the box on the floor between them and took out one of the glasses. An extra tall stem, an over-sized bowl with a distinctive angle.

She twisted the glass in the candlelight, dazzling it like she was waving a wand.

"Beautiful," she said.

"Yes, beautiful." He watched her. Watched the light in her eyes, the play of the glass's reflection on her skin, the way the green silk of her shirt folded at her throat.

"For white wine?" she asked, breaking the spell, switching back to practical matters.

"Yes, for Chardonnay and Chablis."

He took another glass from the box. "See? The shape sends the wine to mid-palate, to capture the aroma, and so you can taste the fruit flavors."

She laughed, a musical sound. "So now you're a wine snob?"

"No," he said. "I was reading the box." He picked up

the corkscrew, opened the wine and poured her a sample. "Taste."

She did. "It's perfect." She held out her glass for more. He filled both their glasses while she ladled out the mac and cheese. As they ate their meal, he told her what Pro had said.

"A *divorce?* Are you sure? But I thought—"

"It doesn't matter that it was not consummated."

"But—"

"Neither of us is . . . physically incapable of sexual relations," he said, repeating Pro's words.

She stared at him a moment. "Right." And then she shook her head. "But . . . a whole year?"

"That's how long it takes." He'd figured she'd be upset about the timing.

"A *year?*"

"A bit longer than that. We have to wait a year before things can be filed. Then it goes fairly quickly."

"I can't believe it." She covered her mouth with both hands.

"Don't worry. Your Aunt Myra won't find out. The only thing that affects you is . . ."

"Is?"

He needed to make sure she knew. "You can't marry Dan during this time."

She scrunched up her nose. "I'm not marrying Dan. Ever."

"Good," he said, happy with the conviction in her voice. "In the meantime, I have to get the marriage certificate."

"Didn't we get it that night?"

"No. It doesn't get filed until later. It should be at the Clark County Recorder's office by Tuesday. I'll phone them then and order a copy." He paused, sipped some wine. "Assuming the documentation is there."

"Why wouldn't it be?" She set down her fork, picked up her wine.

"It should be. It's just that, in case there's a problem, well . . ."

"Just tell me!"

It was hard to admit, even to her. "I can't remember the name of the chapel."

She laughed, relieved. "It was that Elvis chapel somewhere near . . . no . . . maybe it was . . ." She huffed out a long sigh. "There were so many of them."

"And," he said, "I don't remember the name of the officiant."

"I do." She picked up her fork again. "Kris Kringle."

He raised a brow at her.

"Yes, really," she said. "Actually, *Christopher* Kringle. I remember because I thought he was Kris Kringle's brother and I thought it was funny."

"That can't be his real name."

"No, or it could be. He could have changed his name," she said. "Figured it was good for business. Everyone would want to be married by an Elvis impersonator named Kris Kringle."

"Then why not impersonate Kris Kringle?"

"I have no idea," she said. "At any rate, he was a funny Elvis. I think he'd had a few drinks."

At least they had a name, Mark thought. He'd call on Tuesday and order the certificate, and they would get on with their divorce.

Their *divorce*. "I never thought I'd get divorced," he said. "Like my parents."

"I don't think this counts." Emily swirled the wine in her glass, watching the reflections of candlelight. And then, "Have you said anything to Judith?"

"No."

"Have you had a date with her since you got back from

Vegas?"

"Can't."

"Why not?"

"I'm a married man."

She smiled at him. "Will you quit it?"

They finished two servings each of the mac and cheese and then decided to open the chapel package.

First they found a book of poetry by Khalil Gibran, a pack of *I Love You* cards suggesting various things to give each other like back rubs and foot rubs, a box of strawberry-scented condoms, and a sparkly ivory-colored card with a picture of two gold rings on the front.

"I didn't get you a ring," he said.

"You can get me one later," she answered, going along with the game. "What's it say inside?"

She leaned close to him and they read it together.

> *You finally found each other!*
> *Very cool!*
> *Wishing you a wonderful*
> *Happily Ever After!*

"I like that," Emily said. "What else is in here?"

Next they found several noisemakers, a container of heart-shaped chocolates, T-shirts with *Just Married* on the back, and coffee mugs with *Mr.* on one and *Mrs.* on the other.

"Nice," he said. "We can be Mr. & Mrs. Bainbridge. Well, Dr. & Mrs. Bainbridge." A little pause. "Do you want to be Emily Bainbridge?"

"*What?*"

"Until we're divorced," he said, feeling the wine. "Will you be Mrs. Bainbridge?"

"Don't even start," she told him. "You might slip and call me that when someone is around to hear."

"No one is around to hear." Another sip of wine. "That

night," he said, "did you kiss me or did I kiss you?"

"We kissed each other."

"Several times, right?"

"Yes."

"But who started it?"

"I think it was mutual."

"I think it was nice." He looked at her, right into her beautiful blue eyes. "We could try again," he said, leaning toward her. "See if there's anything worth remembering."

An impish smile played over her face and she leaned toward him.

He lightly touched his lips to hers, a featherlight touch, and she didn't pull away. He moved a little closer, a little nibble. Then he touched her face, with one hand, two hands and the next thing he knew he'd pulled her into his lap and she'd wrapped her arms and legs around him.

Heat flooded his body and mind, radiating from the top of his head to his curling toes. He slipped his hands into her hair as he deepened the kiss, and she tightened her hold on him. A wave of dizziness shook him as they fused together, and a strange and powerful disorientation swept him away to a place he'd never known. And always known.

Then his cell rang.

"Damn." Reluctantly, he released his grip on her, but kept her in his lap.

She laughed and nuzzled his neck.

"I need to check this," he said. "It could be the hospital."

He held the phone in front of them, expecting to see some urgent message, something the impressive and talented Dr. Kit Livingston couldn't handle.

Instead, Judith's name popped up, with a strip of pink and white icons representing hearts and kisses. And the words—

I'm here for you if you want to come over now . . .

The world shifted, and Emily slipped out of his arms like a wisp of smoke, like she'd never been there in the first place. Her hair fanned around her shoulders and her eyes shone with a look of hurt.

Sitting a foot away from him on the carpet, she said, "You'd better leave."

Chapter Thirteen

Abnormal temperature trend

Catherine Forsythe rushed into the entrance of the Winward Elementary School, saw the sign that told her to remove her boots, and flinched.

Really?

Her boots were clean. And besides, there were puddles all over that hallway from those children who dripped mud off their coats.

She hated this weather. The Chinooks might bring temporary warmth, but they made a mess of the streets and sidewalks, and this hallway. Bedlam reigned in front of her—high level chatter, along with screaming, or laughing. She wasn't sure.

Straight ahead, she saw the sign that said *Main Office*. Myra had told her Emily's kindergarten classroom was the third door down from the office.

Ignoring the *All Visitors Must Check In* sign, she marched past the Main Office and reached the door that said ECS—not kindergarten.

Why did they have to make things difficult? It was *kindergarten*. It wasn't like these kids could actually learn anything. They were so . . . so . . . small.

Two of them collided with her as she stood in the doorway. Twins. One in blue and one in red. The blue one turned back, took the hand of another, somewhat smaller child, and guided him into the classroom.

Children were scurrying everywhere. Some stuffed coats into colorful lockers near the door. Some climbed all over big plastic cubes. Some were rolling paper off a child-sized artist's easel. And others wandered aimlessly about the room.

Near the windows, Emily and Noelle were standing on a yellow and green checkerboard mat, oblivious to the commotion around them. What was Noelle doing here? Didn't she have her own classroom to organize?

Gesturing with her hands, Noelle was speaking rapidly to Emily—who didn't appear to be listening. In fact, Emily looked exhausted. She looked like she hadn't slept last night, or like she'd lost her best friend.

Suddenly a buzzer sounded, a loud obnoxious noise worse than an alarm clock. And then, music started to play.

Jolly old St. Nicholas
Lean your ear this way.
Don't you tell a single soul
What I'm going to say.

Some of the classrooms still had their doors open. Catherine could hear the child voices singing along with the broadcast Christmas carol. But here, inside the kindergarten classroom, no one was singing along. The music had no effect on these students, if you could call them students. These tiny little children carried on with their random activities, and now all of the paper was off that easel. How did Emily deal with this?

How did Emily deal with anything? If only she would listen to her aunt. Admittedly, her aunt Myra could be a bit overbearing but she had her nieces' best interests at heart. Which was why Catherine was here, trying to help.

Someone needed to convince Noelle to have her wedding at the Country Club. And since Emily was the only one who could do that, Catherine needed to convince Emily.

But it didn't look like they would be able to talk this morning. Not in this zoo.

"Catherine? What are you doing here?"

Noelle had left Emily and was on her way out the door.

"I was going to talk to Emily."

"Not now," Noelle said. "She's working. She needs to settle her students."

Catherine glanced across the room and saw Emily not doing anything to settle her students. Instead, she was standing there, in some yoga pose, not paying any attention to her students at all. Had the woman lost her mind?

Jolly old Saint Nicholas finished playing over the school's PA system, and the noise in the kindergarten room lessened. One by one the children stopped what they were doing, walked to the checkerboard mat and, for some unknown reason, tried to imitate Emily's pose. It was as if she had some Pied Piper effect on them. *Weird.*

"Come to my classroom," Noelle said.

"How come you're not in your classroom?"

"I was lucky. I got a parent volunteer this morning. He's starting things off." And then, "What did you want to talk to Emily about?"

"Stuff for your wedding. It can wait. I'll catch her at her apartment later." They walked down the strangely quiet hallway.

"How was your date with Ryder?" Noelle asked.

"Wonderful," Catherine said. Especially considering how hard it was for Ryder to take time off. And she'd finally convinced him to go to the Pelican's Roost. "He's such a sweetie. But *that friend* of his." Ryder had wanted to go with his friend Logan, and Logan had brought his girlfriend, Cheryl.

They'd reached a door with sparkly green Christmas

trees on it and a sign that said Grade Three. Noelle paused at the door. "What friend?"

"Logan. Do you know him?"

"Yes, Logan. We've met a few times."

"That man has commitment issues."

"Ryder?"

"*Ryder?* Of course not. He doesn't have commitment issues, he's marrying *me*. I'm talking about his friend Logan."

"Oh. Right."

"Logan's girlfriend, Cheryl, is a perfectly lovely woman."

"I haven't met her."

"She's waiting for Logan to pop the question," Catherine said. "The man does not know a good thing when he sees it."

"Catherine, I really have go."

"Yes, yes, of course you do."

Noelle opened the classroom door and Catherine saw a roomful of calm children, nestled all snug in their desks. The desks were arranged in a large circle and in the center of the circle was a lot of straw, and a little lamb.

"You have a lamb in your classroom?"

"Baa," said the lamb.

As the children attempted the tree pose, quiet fell over the classroom, until all that could be heard was the sound of Benjy rustling under the teacher's desk and Chewy running on his wheel.

Emily also tried to quiet her mind, to let go of the images of Saturday night's disaster. Even with all of Sunday and trying to distract herself, she hadn't been able to come to grips with what had happened. She and Mark had gone from the easy camaraderie they'd had since childhood to instantaneous passion. A match had been struck, held to dry tinder, and all her carefully held reserve had gone up in flames.

She tipped out of tree pose.

Stupid, stupid, stupid. It was exactly what she'd feared. The only way she could have Mark in her life was as her friend. As lovers, they would never last.

She couldn't even blame it on the wine. She'd *wanted* to kiss him. She'd *wanted* to relive those stolen moments in Vegas. *Stupid, stupid girl.*

Admit it, she told herself. She had always loved Mark. But watching him grow up, watching him go out with all those women, watching him end all those pseudo relationships—she knew she could never be one of those women. Because she could not risk that inevitable end to the relationship. She could not risk losing him. It would hurt too much. He was her best friend and she couldn't mess with that.

But on Saturday night, she had.

"You're wobbling, Miss Emily," Francine told her.

Emily ignored the child, tried to focus on her breath. *I know I'm breathing in. I know I'm breathing out.* She forced herself to focus . . . to empty her mind, to assume her careful practiced stance.

"Still wobbling," Francine said.

Damn. Emily opened her eyes and settled down into lotus. The children followed her lead.

"This morning we have a special guest," she said.

"Santa?" Ryan asked.

"No, not Santa."

"Santa comes on Christmas Eve," Bobby stated.

"And brings you toys," Allison.

"If you've been good," Francine.

"What if you're bad?" Kelly.

"You're not bad," Emily said.

"But what if—" Kelly's bottom lip quivered.

"You're not bad," Emily said again. "You are good, although sometimes you may have a bad day."

"Like a bad hair day?" Kyle asked.

"Something like that. And now," Emily went on, "I want the paper back on the easel. Then you can do Anything Time."

"And then?" Ryan and Kyle and Allison and Kelly and Bobby asked at once.

"Then our special guest is bringing gingerbread men and we'll decorate them."

"Can we eat them too?" Bobby asked.

That child was always hungry. "You'll each make two," Emily said. "At lunch, you can eat one of them."

An hour later, as planned, Aunt Myra arrived with the gingerbread men and decorating supplies. Actually, there were gingerbread men *and* women. The men had two legs, the women had skirts. Emily had never thought about that. Maybe she should be politically correct and call them gingerbread persons?

"This is my Aunt Myra," Emily gestured, presenting her aunt to the class.

"Good morning, Aunt Myra," the children replied in unison.

Aunt Myra beamed and Emily was glad she'd thought of this. Her aunt liked being useful. In fact, asking Aunt Myra to be a volunteer solved several problems. Emily got help, the children got a project and Aunt Myra was diverted from her meddling with Noelle's wedding.

"You've done a lot of work," Emily said, picking up a gingerbread girl.

"Gingerbread men are one of my specialties."

Ever organized, Aunt Myra had tubes of white, red, and

green icing, all neatly packaged in sets of three so each table could have its own supplies. There were also green and red gumdrops, thin red licorice strings and jars of sprinkles.

As the students sat in the chairs around the tables, Emily and her aunt set out paper plates of gingerbread people. Each child got a boy and a girl. By now, Emily no longer needed to alphabetize the children, but they seemed to like their assigned places. Except for Billy. He'd traded places with Sarah so he could sit beside Tina. And, of course, Benjy remained under the desk.

As Aunt Myra started handing out tubes of icing, and Emily finished passing around the paper plates, the classroom door opened and closed with a loud clonk. Another teacher coming to visit?

Emily turned. And saw Dan.

A chill swept through her, a blast of Arctic air. Wearing a three-piece navy suit and a smug expression, he stood there with his hands in his pockets. "I heard you needed volunteers," he said.

Emily glared at her aunt.

"I thought he could help." Aunt Myra shrugged, hands splayed.

"In kindergarten? He's an accountant. What does he know about kindergarten?"

"He can count out the gumdrops."

Emily cringed. Hot blood burned through her veins. She'd been set up. Again. How could she . . . How could Aunt Myra keep doing this?

"Give me a job," Dan said. "I'm happy to help."

Okay . . . I know I'm breathing in. I know I'm breathing out.

"Is he your boyfriend?" Francine asked.

"No. He's a parent volunteer."

"Whose parent?"

"I have no idea."

"Give everybody one of these," Myra said to Dan as

she filled cupcake wrappers with sprinkles. Dan, good at following instructions, walked around the tables, distributing the sprinkles, and then doing the same for the other components as instructed.

With a happy level of chatter, the children set to work. They traded tubes of icing, carefully spread icing over their cookies, plopped on gumdrop eyes and buttons, lined up the thin licorice to make striped skirts or frizzy hair, and tapped sprinkles wherever they wanted.

"I added a few more guests to the reception," Aunt Myra said.

Emily pressed her fingers to her forehead, hair rising on the back of her neck.

"Friends of the family," Aunt Myra said.

"Noelle wants a small reception. You know that."

"But I don't want anyone to feel left out."

"One of your kids is under your desk," Dan said, sounding amused.

"I know." Emily looked directly into Dan's eyes. "Leave him alone," she said, firmly.

"Kyle ate one of my gumdrops," Ryan squealed.

"I need more buttons," Bobby said with a mouthful, eating as he decorated.

Billy happily gave his gumdrops to Tina.

"He should be sitting at the table," Dan said. "He can't make a gingerbread man if he's under the desk." Dan bent down in front of the desk. "Hi there. My name's Dan. What's your name?"

"We could use the extra room at the Country Club," Aunt Myra continued.

"No." *Poor Noelle.*

"If only I could convince Noelle to have it at the Country Club," Aunt Myra went on. "You should help me. It's your fault she has bad associations with the place."

"*My* fault?"

"We should have had your rehearsal dinner somewhere else."

"What's a hearsal?" Francine asked.

Emily swung around to face Aunt Myra. "Don't you understand? Noelle wants a small affair. And you already have thirty guests."

"A few more than that," Aunt Myra said. "They will barely fit in the living room. It's ridiculous and—"

A loud piercing scream resounded over the classroom, and most likely into the hall, and everywhere.

Emily turned in time to see Dan pulling Benjy out from under the desk. Keith and Brian tipped out of their chairs and rushed to the scene.

Flailing his arms and legs, Benjy struggled to get out of Dan's hold. Keith and Brian each kicked one of Dan's shins, forcing him to let go of Benjy.

Dan hopped away from the twins. "Ouch!" He rubbed his shins. "Emily! Can't you control these little monsters?!"

Benjy scooted back under the desk. Keith and Brian stood in front of it, arms folded.

Still rubbing his shins, Dan looked confused. "I was trying to help."

Emily stomped over to where he stood, and pointed to the door. "Out."

"What? You can't throw me out."

"I can. Get out." She pointed again.

"Now Emily, calm down," Aunt Myra said. "It's all a misunderstanding."

"You too."

"What?"

"Aunt Myra. Leave. At once."

With his Santa hat askew, Mr. Valentine rushed through the door. "I heard a scream."

"Mr. Valentine," Emily said.

"Call me—"

"Make these people leave."

Mrs. Mistle arrived in the next moment, did a quick glance about the room. Her hands went to her hips, and her expression grew stern.

"If you would please come with me," Mr. Valentine said. "I'm sure we can sort this out."

"Oh honestly, you can't be serious." Aunt Myra attempted a weak smile.

"You heard the man," Mrs. Mistle said. "Get a move on."

"Goodbye, Aunt Myra," Emily said.

"Goodbye, Aunt Myra," the children said in unison.

Chapter Fourteen

Frankincense and Myrrh

On Wednesday morning, Mark sat at the back of the hospital cafeteria with Pro, drinking the standard issue coffee.

"*Nothing* at the Clark County Recorder's office?" Pro asked. Again.

"It should have been there yesterday. It wasn't. I phoned again first thing this morning. Still nothing."

"Then it's time to start phoning chapels," Pro told him. "You don't want the paperwork to get lost."

"I know."

"And you haven't remembered which chapel?"

"No."

"Have you asked Emily?"

"Yes. She doesn't remember either." And he didn't want her worrying about it. He wanted to help her, somehow, because now, more than ever, that beautiful woman was messing with his head.

He couldn't stop thinking about her, about kissing her, and then seeing the hurt look in her eyes when Judith had sent that text.

Worse, Emily wasn't answering *his* texts, or phone calls. Or her apartment buzzer. He was beginning to feel like Dan, stalking her.

"Well? Have you?" Pro interrupted his thoughts.

"Pardon?"

"I said, have you told Judith about Vegas?"

"No."

"Have you even seen Judith since you got back from Vegas?"

"Yes. Saturday night. I dropped by." He'd headed straight to Judith's apartment as soon as he'd left Emily.

"That's it? Dropped by?"

"I took her out to the Keg. Nice dinner."

"I see," Pro said, sitting back in his chair, folding his arms.

"You see what?"

Pro shrugged, gave a small smile. "Expensive restaurant. Expensive dinner. You sat in the middle of the restaurant?"

"Yes," Mark answered, knowing where his friend was going with this.

"Hard for her to make a scene that way."

"She didn't make a scene." And she hadn't, not really. She'd been a little snippy. Nothing serious.

"You broke up with her."

"It was time."

"You need to settle down," Pro said.

"So do you."

On Thursday morning, as Emily walked to school on the dry sidewalk, she gazed at the eastern sky—a clear sky with a band of light orange at the horizon. Sunrise in half an hour. Most of the stars had become invisible and there was no moon. The moon would not rise until later in the day.

A week ago, the moon was a thin waxing crescent. So today, the moon should be at first quarter, or close to it. Right now, the sky was empty.

This morning, she'd received another text from Mark. She still didn't know how to respond. Not yet. Not until she somehow sorted out how she would deal with . . . with this . . . this loving him, and not being able to love him. But she couldn't think about it because she needed to focus all her energy on her sister and prepare for the wedding. In another week, it would be Christmas Eve, and Noelle and Troy would be married.

At Noelle's shower, Frank had casually mentioned there would be a full moon on Christmas Eve. He'd even gone so far as to suggest that the wedding party move outside to watch the moonrise.

Of course, Aunt Myra had been appalled. *Everyone would have to dress up in warm coats and boots!* And then, Aunt Myra had changed the topic to her Country Club and how much better a venue it was than their living room.

Since Monday's incident, Aunt Myra had been phoning and Emily had not been answering. So Aunt Myra had resorted to sending texts.

However, her aunt did not own a cell phone and she didn't want one. She was a holdout for land lines. That was how she got in touch. She also hated answering machines and expected people to pick up on the first ring.

As a workaround, Aunt Myra had borrowed Frank's cell and had learned how to send text messages. Emily had received quite a few. Cheerful things, like—

> *You really need to grow up!!!*

And . . .

> *You must come to your senses and find a way to move the reception to the Country Club!!!*

And . . .

> *There is NO SNOW in the forecast. What's the use of a Christmas Eve wedding if there is no snow???!!!*

It was good that her aunt was learning to text. Maybe she'd buy her own cell phone someday. And maybe someday, Aunt Myra would give up trying to run everything her way.

If only.

Walking along the sidewalk, Emily stepped around some branches that had fallen from the poplars—those big indigenous trees that grew well in Calgary, but were not shy about littering yards and sidewalks with their debris.

Emily could hardly believe she'd stood up to her aunt. Because where Aunt Myra was concerned, Emily had always backed down. The same way she'd backed down six months ago, and worn the purple chiffon dress—that she didn't like.

At the last minute, Aunt Myra had decided the purple chiffon dress was *the* dress for the occasion. The dress that absolutely must be worn for the rehearsal party.

Emily had been sitting at the large round table between Dan and Noelle. Noelle had Troy on her other side. And Dan had Aunt Myra on his other side. They'd almost finished dinner, dessert was still to come, and then the blocking out of the steps for the ceremony would follow.

Emily shifted in her chair. The purple chiffon itched and chafed her skin. The last minute dress. She'd tried not to think about it, about the dress, and how it wasn't what she wanted to wear. She'd tried to focus on the fact that she was marrying Dan, moving out of the house and getting on with her life.

And no, she wasn't wildly in love with Dan, but then she'd never met anyone who made her feel that way. But she did like Dan. He never had arguments with Aunt Myra, and Aunt Myra approved of him.

Unlike Frank and Mark. Aunt Myra did not approve of them. Instead, they were the bane of her existence. It was a miracle she'd put them on the guest list for the wedding and for tonight's party. But she had, and she was even sitting beside Frank. Mark was next to his father, and Judith was next to Mark.

That night, as Emily sat there in her scratchy dress, she overheard Dan talking to Aunt Myra. She couldn't hear the conversation, but the two were head to head in some important discussion.

Across the table, Mark had sat with Judith. He was laughing loudly about something while Judith, not laughing, clutched his arm in a death grip.

Emily heard enough to know Frank was telling a joke—something about a surgeon walking into a bar—and Troy and Noelle were waiting for the punch line. As the babble of conversations went on around her, Emily saw her life flash before her ... all organized and structured and on course. And safe.

At that moment Dan huffed out a breath and dropped his fork on his plate. He reached for his wine, gulped down the half-full glass. Then he pushed his chair back and stood. A second later he was heading for the door, moving quickly, with purpose.

She didn't know what to make of it, but an unease settled over her. "I'll be right back," she told her sister, and she followed Dan out of the elaborately decorated room.

She found him in the Country Club garden near the pond, sitting on a bench, staring at the water. The fairy lights reflected weakly off the surface.

A horn tooted, shaking Emily from the past to the present. She'd reached the school parking lot and Mrs. Mistle, the school secretary, was pulling in and waving at her.

Mrs. Mistle got out of her car and joined Emily on the sidewalk. "I have an idea," Mrs. Mistle said. "For the Christmas concert."

Emily looked up at the sky. "They're kindergarten

students. They don't need to perform." And never mind the students, Emily did not want to perform.

"But they'll feel left out."

"There's no way I'll get Benjy to stand up in front of everyone. *He* will feel left out."

"He can sit with his grandmother."

His grandmother? That would be nice, but hopefully his parents were coming too. Because Emily needed to talk to his parents and figure out why he was hiding under the desk.

"It will be perfect," Mrs. Mistle said, as they walked to the school entrance. "The children can sing Jingle Bells. The way they do with Howie."

With Mr. *Call me Howie* Valentine. "I'll think about it," Emily said.

Mark finished his call to the seventh chapel on the list. No one had heard of Christopher Kringle, the wedding officiant who had married them. Mark was starting to wonder if the man even existed.

Before entering the next number, he thought about sending another text to Emily. She'd probably ignore it. The same way she'd ignored every other text he'd sent.

"Dr. Bainbridge?" A nurse with a name tag that said *Roberta, RN* stood next to him. "Bloodwork is back on 3C," she said. "I think you'd better have a look."

After lunch, the students returned from the playground, put their boots on the mat outside the classroom door, put their coats in their cubbies and took out their little blankets. Most of them were tired but they wouldn't nap until they'd heard the next installment of "Charlie's Christmas Eve Adventure".

Emily opened the book and started to read aloud. As usual, they listened, enthralled, and Benjy listened too, as he peeked through the slats under the teacher's desk.

In today's story, Charlie and the other little warthogs had escaped from the evil stepmother. They'd all piled into an old sleigh and were heading home. But it was snowing so hard, Charlie couldn't see which way to go.

At the end of the chapter, Emily quietly closed the book and without any prompting, the children settled down on the mat for a long winter's nap, and quickly fell asleep.

Emily walked to the teacher's desk and checked on Benjy. He'd fallen asleep, hugging his teddy bear, but he didn't have his blanket. There was only one blanket left in the cubbies—an old red blanket with a patchwork edging that was frayed.

She shook out the little blanket, brought it to the child, and covered him up.

Friday afternoon arrived, and the school week ended with a flurry of mitts and boots and hats and coats. The twins helped Benjy get into his outdoor clothes and brought him to the bus.

The sound of Chewy running on his wheel reminded her to feed the gerbil. Since she'd taken over in the ECS, the students had remained concerned about Chewy's health. They watched him, but kept a good distance from his cage. Some of them still asked if he would die. Emily shook her head. No doubt, they watched too much television, or at least, inappropriate television.

Classroom in order, Emily got her coat and headed home to her apartment. The Chinook winds gusted over the streets swirling the leftover autumn leaves into the air and spinning them into the darkening sky. Soon, she reached Winward Groves. She fobbed her key card and let herself into the building.

When she got off the elevator on the seventh floor, she spotted the long white box next to her door and felt like kicking it. But, after a couple of deep breaths, she opened it.

Long-stemmed red roses. He was back to red roses. Moving aside the tissue paper, she found the card which, instead of the usual *Dan*, had more writing on it this time. She held up the expensive parchment and read:

> *You must know that you hurt your aunt's feelings and you embarrassed her. I understand that you are stressed because of your sister's wedding and I forgive you. I'm sure that when you apologize to your aunt, she will forgive you too.*
>
> *As always,*
> *love,*
> *Dan*

A couple of rips and she tossed the pieces of paper into her purse. Then she picked up the box and headed for Mrs. Harcourt's door.

Mrs. Harcourt answered on the first knock. "Still trying?" she asked.

"He is," Emily said. "Very trying."

Mrs. Harcourt exchanged the roses for a jar of pumpkin soup and two freshly baked croissants.

After returning to her own apartment, Emily set the soup to simmer, and took a bath. And then she felt much better. She felt even better after she'd eaten some soup and a croissant.

Sitting there, she spotted her camera, still on the countertop where Mark had left it last Saturday. She needed to delete those pictures. Soon. Except, a part of her wanted to see them.

And another part didn't. How could she look at those pictures, knowing she might have become another in Mark's long string of relationships that never went anywhere. Their friendship would not survive a love affair.

Maybe their friendship was already over.

A knock sounded on her door.

She jumped. Her pulse raced. If that was Dan again . . . She gritted her teeth.

A voice, muffled by the heavy door, said, "Hello?" A female voice.

Noelle? Emily checked the peephole. Sure enough it was Noelle.

"I didn't bother buzzing," Noelle said. "I knew you wouldn't answer."

"What's wrong?"

"Everything." Noelle entered the apartment. "What's that smell? Did you cook? It smells great."

"Mrs. Harcourt's pumpkin soup."

"Mrs. Harcourt?" Noelle tilted her head. "More roses?"

"Yes."

"Wow." Noelle hung her coat in the closet. "Even after you threw him out of your classroom. That guy is determined."

"Disillusioned."

"Got any more soup?"

"Yes. And a homemade croissant," Emily said. "Would you like some Chardonnay?"

"I would love some."

While Noelle ladled out a bowl of soup, Emily headed for glasses. Lined up beside the tumblers, Mark's wine glasses glistened with a bright sheen. She carefully lifted out two.

"Aunt Myra has booked the Swan Room at the Country Club," Noelle said, as she sat at the counter with her soup and the other croissant. "Frank told me."

"Frank?"

"He was visiting again. He likes Aunt Myra's baking." Noelle sipped her soup. "He hates the new tile floor though. Too bad for him." Another sip of soup. "Anyway, after he was done complaining about the floor, he told me Aunt Myra has booked the Swan Room and she intends to have the reception there and I'd better get used to the idea since, he said, and I quote, *there is no stopping Myra!*"

Emily poured the wine, watching the golden liquid swirl in the crystal, remembering all those times Aunt Myra had charged ahead with *her* plans for both of them.

Picking up one of the glasses, Noelle said, "These are from Mark."

Emily nodded.

"You should have opened these a long time ago."

"I should have." Emily tasted the wine, licked her lips and gave it a thumbs up. "Aunt Myra can't do that. She knows you want a small wedding and you want it by the fireplace."

"She knows. But she's been planning for the Country Club all along. Oh, Em. What if she tells all the guests to meet us there? What if Troy and I have to go to the Country Club because she's sent everyone there?"

"We could phone everyone on the guest list and tell them to come to the house?"

"But I don't even know who's on the guest list anymore. She keeps adding to it."

"If they weren't on the original list, it doesn't matter."

"I am so sick of this." Noelle sighed, her shoulders drooping. "She wants it to be her perfect wedding. *Your* wedding was supposed to be the perfect one and now it's up to me." Noelle twisted the stem of her glass, watching the wine spin. "Maybe I'll walk out at the last moment like you did."

Right, Emily thought. It had been a horrible night. And a difficult decision . . . and yet not.

She saw Dan sitting on the bench beside the pond in the Country Club garden, obviously upset about something.

And she was nervous. Nothing specific, but she remembered wondering if it was normal wedding nervousness. And then wondering if it was normal to be nervous? Was that the way weddings were supposed to be?

"Is something wrong?" she'd asked him.

"What do you think?"

Her muscles tensed. The same as they'd been doing all day. Pre-wedding butterflies? Wasn't that how it should be for such a big decision? One that was so . . . so . . . final. *Till death do us part.*

"I can't stand that you wore that dress," he'd said, finally. "We agreed on the yellow one."

What? He was upset about her dress? "I know I said the yellow one, but Aunt Myra wanted—"

"Yes, *Myra* wanted it. But what about *me?* I wanted the yellow one. It was supposed to complement my tie."

For a second, Emily wondered if she had heard correctly. "Your *tie?*"

"You let your aunt talk you into that. Now you've ruined my evening."

She slowly sat down, about a foot away from him on the hard concrete bench.

"All Myra cares about is you. The bride. She's making such a big deal about the bride. But what about me? No one ever thinks of the groom." He picked up speed, counting off complaints on his fingers. "I went along with the menu, and the flowers, and the gold invitations. I'm tired of everything being Myra's way."

Emily listened, knots forming in her stomach. "I thought you agreed with all those things."

"I didn't!"

No? Until that moment, she'd thought Dan could stand up to Aunt Myra. That was one of the things that had attracted her to him in the first place. In fact, that was the biggest thing that had attracted her to him. Of course, there were a lot of things she liked about him—he was good-looking, he was usually easy going, he had a lot of friends. And, he could stand up to Aunt Myra. No one else could.

Except, of course, Mark and Frank.

"I hate this stupid rehearsal." Dan grimaced. "Your aunt is going to insist that everyone stand in exactly the right place." His hands fisted and his voice rose. "I need you to pay more attention to me. If you loved me, you would pay more attention to me. No one ever pays attention to the groom. The focus is always on the bride."

She looked at him, like she was seeing him for the first time. And then it hit her. At that moment . . . as she sat beside him in front of the still waters of the pond . . . with the fairy lights all around them.

She didn't love him.

She'd thought she was moving on with her life by getting married. It had felt like it was time to get married, but, she didn't love him. Somehow that New Year's Eve proposal had started her on this trip down the rabbit hole, pushing her in a direction she didn't want to go.

"You're right," she said.

"Of course I'm right!" A slight pause, a lowered voice. "Right about what?"

"I don't love you."

"Oh damn it." He raked his fingers through his hair. "Look, I'm sorry I upset you."

"You didn't upset me." And he hadn't. He had simply jolted her back to reality.

"Stop being silly. You love me. Now let's go back inside and get this stupid rehearsal over with." He got to his feet and reached for her.

"No."

"*What?*" He sat down again. "I said I was sorry. I'm

feeling the strain of your aunt's manipulations, that's all."

"I can't marry you."

He stared at her, his forehead wrinkled. "You—you don't mean that."

"Yes, I do."

"Emily. There's a roomful of people in there." He used his best patronizing voice. "You can't walk out now."

"You can tell them."

He frowned. "Tell them what?"

"Wedding canceled."

She stood and turned to leave, not sure where she was going to go.

"Oh grow up for God's sake! You're acting like a spoiled child!"

She spun around then, faced him, and squared her shoulders. "Thank you for letting me see my mistake, Dan, by complaining about my dress."

He jumped to his feet, a hint of panic touched his features. "You can't cancel. You'd break your aunt's heart. Think of all the work she's put into this!"

Emily took a step back from him. Guilt. Was he trying to guilt her into marrying him?

"No! Listen! Damn it! So we're having a spat." He moved closer. "We've never fought before. All couples do. But you had to choose tonight for your big argument." He grabbed her wrist and tugged.

She twisted away from him and started running, back up the path toward the main building. Near the arbor, she saw Mark. Her constant Mark. When she reached him, she took hold of his hands and, stuttering, she asked him to drive her home.

Home, to Aunt Myra's. Two weeks later, she'd found the apartment, and she'd moved.

At the time, it had seemed like all the order in her universe had collapsed. She had felt so stupid for not recognizing the signs earlier. For taking so long to figure out that marrying Dan could never work.

"You're back there," Noelle said.

"Yes, I was remembering that night. Rehearsal night."

Noelle nodded at her wine. "Whatever he said, or did, it must have been huge for you to change your mind at the zero hour."

"That's just it," Emily said. "It wasn't huge."

"It wasn't?"

"It was about my dress."

Noelle raised her eyebrows. "Your dress? The purple one?" Squinting, she seemed to go back in time to that night. "I remember you wanted to wear the yellow one. And then you changed your mind."

"Aunt Myra changed *her* mind. She decided she wanted me to wear the purple one. And Dan didn't like that dress."

Noelle thought about that. "Makes sense," she said.

And Emily thought it made about as much sense as anything.

"I had a feeling it wouldn't work with Dan," Noelle told her sister.

"You did?"

"Right when he proposed to you."

They laughed.

"It was supposed to be romantic," Noelle said.

"It was cheesy."

"It was New Year's Eve." Noelle rotated the wine bottle so she could see the label, the swirly letters contained inside the silver embossed border. "Big fancy dinner, everybody laughing and happy. Then he gets down on one knee at the table and shows you that diamond." She tilted her head, a whimsical look. "What would have happened if you'd said no?"

"I wish I had."

"But you didn't say no. But then, you didn't say yes

either. You didn't say anything. Dan slid that ring on your finger and it was a done deal."

"I couldn't speak. I remember thinking there was something wrong with me. I remember thinking I had trouble making a commitment."

"Oh, Em. When the right guy comes along, you won't hesitate for a second. You'll know. And you'll marry him in an instant."

And she had. In Las Vegas.

"But did you have to wait till the rehearsal dinner to come to your senses?"

Emily laughed. "I guess I did."

"You should have known, right when he insisted you quit your job at the high school."

"He wanted the three month honeymoon."

"But you didn't."

"I don't think I knew what I wanted." It had been such a muddled, lonely time.

"Too bad you quit your job."

"Yes, but—" She paused, smiled. "I'm actually liking ECS."

Noelle smiled, too. "I'm not surprised. You're good at it," she said. "You're good at anything you set your mind to."

"Thanks."

"It's true. You're good at what you do."

"Just never good enough for Aunt Myra."

They sat there, at the counter, looking into the little kitchen with its bleak overhead light.

"Why do we do everything she wants?" Noelle frowned at her rhetorical question.

"Because we always have. Ever since she became our guardian. Well, ever since she got sick that time."

A beat of silence followed. "Maybe we were afraid," Noelle went on, "that if we didn't do what she wanted . . ." She left the thought unfinished.

"That, if we didn't do what she wanted, she'd leave too."

Noelle stared into her wine. "It's what a child would think."

It was. Emily had been nine years old. Noelle had been seven. "We'd lost our parents. We didn't want to lose her too."

"Yeah. Something like that," Noelle said.

"And foster care . . . that sucked."

"Yes, it did."

"We're not little children anymore," Emily said, a sudden surge of self-confidence emerging.

"No, we're not," Noelle agreed. "She can't run our lives."

"Or ruin them."

Noelle stared down at her wine, for a couple of moments, and then she held up the crystal wine glass. "To growing up," she said.

"To growing up," Emily answered, clinking glasses with her sister.

Chapter Fifteen

Jingle all the way

The next day, Saturday morning, Emily had wanted to sleep in, but she couldn't. Too many things kept going through her mind. With no specific training for the job, she'd been an ECS teacher for two weeks, and now she was responsible for twenty-four little students.

A heavy responsibility. And, for the most part, things were going well with the class. On Tuesday, she'd meet Benjy's grandmother and hopefully his parents too, and they'd talk about the little boy. Emily didn't want to worry about him, but she did. And she worried about the Christmas concert and what to do about it.

On top of that, her sister's wedding was five days away. Aunt Myra continued to send text messages on Frank's cell: little reminders, subtle lectures, and not so subtle complaints about how Emily was not pulling her weight with the wedding preparations.

The texts from Mark had stopped. She didn't know if that was a good thing or a bad thing. But, they'd see each other at the wedding on Christmas Eve. They would deal with the awkwardness then. And it would definitely be awkward seeing Judith there as Mark's plus one.

She shook her head. No use thinking about something she couldn't change. Instead, she busied herself with cleaning her apartment. Which didn't take long. Her apartment was the size of a postage stamp and not a lot to clean. So she decided to organize the fridge.

Except that was also a quick job, since there was nothing more than a container of cottage cheese, an apple, some milk, a jar of peanut butter and the rest of the wine from last night's visit with Noelle.

Someday, she'd quit storing the peanut butter in there. For now, it gave her a minute sense of being in charge of her destiny—because Aunt Myra hated it when Emily put the peanut butter in the fridge.

She sighed. Not good. Not good at all. To rely on peanut butter for a sense of controlling her destiny.

She sighed again, closed the fridge door, and crossed the living room to find her phone and look at today's weather.

Still no snow in the forecast—too bad for Aunt Myra. Outside, a cold wind blew over the land, sifting and swirling twigs and dead leaves, and scattering them into forlorn little heaps. She should walk to the grocery store and get some eggs and bread and butter. If she bundled up, she'd be warm enough.

Maybe later. For now, she turned around and looked across the room at her camera, sitting on the counter, taunting her.

All right, she told herself. She would deal with those pictures. She'd delete them and clear away that part of her life.

She retrieved the camera and sat on her yoga bolster with her computer on the makeshift table. A few minutes later, the computer had booted up. She inserted the SD card, highlighted everything, and prepared to hit the delete key.

Squeezing her eyes shut, she hesitated. Mark would have seen these pictures. She was almost sure of that. So, she should have a look. She might as well know what he'd seen. And then she could gauge how embarrassed she should be when she saw him again. And anyway, what could it hurt?

Folder open, the wash of colors filled the screen. They'd taken a lot of photos of lots of different things— landmarks, neon signs, perfect strangers and, for some reason, sidewalk squares.

Why was she taking pictures of the sidewalk? But then, why was she taking pictures of strangers? Or were these pictures that Mark had taken as the camera was passed around?

There were also shots of hood ornaments, menus, engagement rings, Elvis bobble heads, an enormous fruit basket and several angles of a guttering candle.

And people. Dozens of photos of people. Most of them strangers, but there were pictures of her. And pictures of Mark. And pictures of both of them standing close together, their arms wrapped around each other. Like the other night. Her stomach clenched.

Obviously, these photos were taken by people they'd found who'd been happy to assist in documenting the night. There were also group shots. People crowding into the frame, giving them the thumbs up.

Scrolling down, she found several shots of an overflowing bottle of champagne, and then other shots of champagne flutes raised high. And there, in that photo, was the officiant, Christopher Kringle, posing with them. In another photo, he was caught mid-laugh as he performed the ceremony.

She hadn't noticed what Christopher Kringle was wearing that night but, seeing the photo now, she thought he didn't have much of an Elvis outfit. In fact, what he wore looked more like a waiter's uniform.

Her attention fell on the closeups of Mark. He had a glow in his eyes that said all was right with the world. Dear

Mark, her friend, her very best friend.

Alone in her living room, with the cold wind blowing outside, she shivered and tugged her sweater tightly around her shoulders. He could never love her, not the way she loved him. But if they could at least remain friends. Tears suddenly welled behind her eyelids. God, she hoped she hadn't ruined everything. If she had, she'd be more alone than ever.

It had been a week since he'd been at her apartment, and they'd been sitting in this exact spot. He'd kissed her, and she'd been transported back to that impossible time when for a brief moment, they were a couple. And then Judith's message had pinged on Mark's phone, and the magic had evaporated.

They could move on. They could forget anything had happened. The same way he'd forgotten they'd even kissed in Las Vegas.

On the plane home, he'd said he didn't remember them kissing in Vegas. But she remembered. Closing her eyes, she wanted to go back, feel that excitement again, that sense of belonging with someone. No, not just someone. With Mark.

A deep ache grew in her chest. Mark didn't even remember, but she did. She would never forget that night. And she didn't want to.

Quickly, before she changed her mind, she created a folder and dragged the photos, all of them, onto her computer.

Maybe later, she would come to her senses and delete them. For now though, she needed to clear the SD card and put it back in her camera, ready for new pictures of a different wedding on Christmas Eve.

Glancing up from her computer, she noticed the crystal unicorn on the top bookshelf. It glinted at her with a wicked look in its glassy eye.

It was time to deal with the unicorn. She found the box and the tissue paper that had wrapped Mark's wine glasses. And then she carefully wrapped the unicorn, the impossible creature. On Christmas Eve, she would return it to Aunt Myra.

With another hour to go, his Sunday shift was almost finished. Mark walked into the coffee room beside the ER. Kit had brewed a pot of his special blend and Pro was pouring a cup.

"Coffee?" Pro asked.

"Please," Mark answered, automatically. He collapsed onto the couch, thinking about the blood gas results on the new admission and the low potassium on the guy in 6A. When Pro handed him a mug of coffee, his brain shifted and he realized Pro was in the wrong place. "What are you doing here?"

"I need a break from working on bylaws," Pro said.

"You do bylaws?"

"Not usually." Pro got coffee for himself. "Remember I told you Aunt Tizzy joined a knitting club?"

"Yeah . . ."

"And she's on the board of directors?"

"Yeah . . ."

Pro's shoulders dropped. "Often," he said, with a heavy sigh, "when a new board is elected, they feel the need to change the bylaws."

"Is that necessary?"

"To some extent." Pro took a gulp of coffee. "But not in this case. They're overthinking what might go wrong and trying to plan for every eventuality. They've lost sight of why they formed the group in the first place."

"Which is?"

Pro shrugged. "To knit."

"Right," Mark said. "Seems simple enough." If only everything could be that simple. But then, people would still find a way to make it *not* simple. To complicate the uncomplicated. To confuse the issue when—

"Have you?" Pro asked.

"Pardon?"

"Have you tracked down the chapel?"

"No. Not yet. I haven't had time."

"Make a list of all the chapels in Vegas," Pro said. "Get Emily to help you phone."

Not going to happen. "Emily is busy."

"Not so busy, she can't—wait a minute. What do you mean, Emily is busy?"

"I mean . . ."

Pro waited.

Mark slumped on the couch, let out a long tired breath. "I mean she's not answering my calls."

"Why not?"

Because I kissed her. Because I went right back to our time in Vegas. Because . . . Judith texted. "Long story."

"Good," Pro said, cradling his coffee mug. "You're having an argument."

What the hell? "Why is that good?"

"It's communication."

"It's . . . complicated." Why did it have to be complicated? Mark blew out a sigh. "This divorce thing could destroy us."

"So." Pro looked at his coffee, studied it. "Don't divorce her."

"I can't marry her."

"You already did."

"But we can't stay married. Marriage doesn't work."

"Mark." Pro bent, and looked him in the eye. "I'm a lawyer, not a psychiatrist. But I'm also your friend. I know marriage didn't work for your parents, but they weren't the right people for each other."

"It's not like that."

"It is. And—I'm just sayin'—if you've found the right person, don't let her go."

Could he ever let her go? It had almost killed him when she'd got engaged to that idiot, Dan. He'd known that Dan was all wrong for her, but he hadn't known what to do about it. But now?

Mark looked away from Pro's knowing gaze. When had he become so freaking transparent?

"Put Kit in charge," Pro said, eyeing Kit as he entered the coffee room.

"What'd I miss?" Kit asked.

"I'm sure Dr. Livingston is capable of running the ER for a few hours while you straighten things out."

Emily entered the quiet classroom. She dropped her purse on top of the teacher's desk and moved aside the teacher's chair so Benjy could easily crawl into his hiding place. With the chair placed against the wall, she sat and looked across the room at the yellow and green checkerboard mat. The shelves behind the mat were neatly filled with storybooks ready for reading. To her left, the teacher's desk was clear except for Mrs. Jannie's notebook. Emily had left it there, although she hardly referred to it at this point.

After a lonely weekend of not knowing whether she wanted to see Mark, or not, Monday morning had finally arrived, and she was acutely aware she needed to pump herself up, and somehow get into the Christmas spirit. For the children's sake.

Out in the hallway, the commotion rose. *There arose such a clatter*, she thought, amused as she pictured *the prancing and pawing* of each little foot. At least she was getting her mind in the game. She needed to, since the day would start in about ten minutes.

Abandoning the teacher's chair, she walked to the first round table and sat on one of the child-sized chairs.

The door opened, and closed, and Noelle trudged into the classroom. Without saying anything, she pulled out another little chair and sat down, too.

"How are you holding up?" Emily asked.

"It's Monday. I'm supposed to get married on Thursday. In Aunt Myra's perfect wedding."

"Aunt Myra needs to get married," Emily mused.

"Yeah. If only we could find someone to marry her." Noelle put her hands on the table, and then dropped her head onto her hands, tapping her head, once, twice, three times.

"That bad?"

Noelle sat up. "I told Troy about her Country Club plans. He is unimpressed. So am I. I'm going to elope."

Emily shook her head. "No. You can't. Tomorrow is the concert and then school is over. We have Wednesday to ourselves. We'll think of something then."

"Right," Noelle said, and then quickly added, "Are you ready for the Christmas concert?" An obvious attempt to change the subject.

"No. But the children want to sing Jingle Bells. With hand motions, apparently. Like they're ringing bells."

"Mr. Valentine's version?"

"Yes."

Noelle considered the idea. "So let them. You don't need to do anything."

"Are you kidding me? I need to get all of them up on the stage and in some kind of order."

"Just don't alphabetize them." Noelle laughed. "But no, don't worry about it. Mr. Valentine and Mrs. Mistle can get them into their places. It will be fine."

"Maybe," Emily said. Except Benjy wouldn't participate. He might not even leave the classroom. He might not even come to school tomorrow.

From the top of the teacher's desk, Emily's cell phone rang with a series of arpeggios, the signal for a call.

"Probably Aunt Myra. Now she's phoning. She usually sends texts." Emily went to check.

Noelle followed her. "Frank has been really good about letting her use his phone. It's a miracle."

Emily checked the readout. Not Aunt Myra, but Mark. Why was he phoning now? At five minutes to nine? Not that she would have picked up anyway.

She swiped the screen, canceling the call.

"Mark?" Noelle stood next to her. "How come you're not answering?"

"No time," Emily said, as the classroom door opened and her students started to come inside.

Taking that as her cue, Noelle said, "See you at lunch," and she was gone.

The morning flew by, progressing from Anything Time, to craft time, to an exciting discussion of tomorrow's concert and finally to some calming yoga poses.

"Can we talk about what we want for Christmas?" Francine asked.

"Maybe after lunch," Emily said, although she didn't like the idea of talking about Christmas presents. What if one of them wanted something they could not have?

Eager to play outside, the children hurried through lunch. The twins brought Benjy his outdoor clothing and in about ten minutes, the classroom was empty and quiet—except for Chewy doing laps on his squeaky wheel.

In the staffroom, Emily sat next to her sister but they didn't have time to talk about Aunt Myra or Aunt Myra's

Country Club plans, since all the talk was about tomorrow's concert.

Mr. Valentine thought Jingle Bells was a wonderful idea and he told Emily that he and Mrs. *Call her Ivy* Mistle would handle everything.

Having seen Mrs. Mistle in action a few times, Emily wasn't so sure about that.

At one o'clock, everyone returned to their classroom and Emily's students were so tired, they had a nap—without having story time.

Forty-five minutes later, a few eyes opened, blankets were shuffled, and soon everyone was sitting up and looking refreshed.

Always persistent Francine asked, "Are we going to talk about what we're getting for Christmas?"

It seemed like they would have to. "Yes, we can talk about that."

"But read first!" several of the children said at once.

And so Emily read the last chapter of "Charlie's Christmas Eve Adventure" in which Charlie and the other little warthogs had to take an unexpected route through the forest. They needed some help from the Christmas fairies in the woods. But, finally, they traveled a good league until they reached the forest fence and arrived home in time for Christmas.

As Emily closed the book, Kelly asked, "What's a league?"

"That's how far they had to go to get home," Allison said.

"A league is about three miles," Emily told them.

"Then why don't they just say three miles?" Billy asked.

The questions stopped when they heard the classroom door open and all eyes turned in that direction.

Accompanied by Makita—Frank's Labradoodle—Mark entered the classroom. He wore his navy blue winter coat but he'd removed his boots. As he stood by the door holding Makita's leash, Mrs. Mistle rushed into the room.

"Sir!"

"Mark," he said, gazing down at the old woman.

"Mark," she repeated, and then, looking up at him, she frowned. "Mark who?"

"Mark Bainbridge."

"Well!" She drew herself up as tall as she could and folded her arms, preparing for a lecture. "Mr. Bainbridge!"

"Dr. Bainbridge," he said, quietly.

"Oh!" She blinked, not expecting the doctor part. "Well, Dr. Bainbridge, you can't have that dog in the school."

"It's my seeing eye dog," Mark told her, with a perfectly serious face.

"Oh!" Mrs. Mistle had apparently not expected that either. Her hands dropped to her sides. "Oh, I'm sorry."

"That's all right," Mark said, touching Mrs. Mistle's arm in that reassuring way of his. "Mostly, I just need her for driving."

Mark's touch must have had the usual effect, since Mrs. Mistle appeared reassured. "All right then," she said. "Carry on." And she left the classroom.

Mark watched the door close, and then he asked, "Is she your principal?"

"School secretary," Emily said. "What are you doing here?"

"My dad told me you were looking for volunteers."

Of course he did.

"Whose father is he?" Tina asked.

"That's a nice dog," Kyle said.

"We were going to talk about what we are getting for Christmas," Francine prompted.

Oh, Mark, why are you here? She looked at the children and back to Mark again, random thoughts whirling through her head.

"I want a dog for Christmas just like that one," Brian stated.

Brian's Christmas wish brought her to attention. She cleared her throat, straightened and gestured to Mark. "You can sit there," she said, indicating the chair next to the teacher's desk, where Benjy peeked out at Makita.

Mark sat on the teacher's chair, and Makita settled between the chair and the desk, with her head on her paws.

The students fidgeted on the checkerboard mat, waiting for the exercise to begin.

Unable to help herself, Emily stole another glance at Mark, who relaxed on the chair, his hands in his lap. Makita seemed to be sleeping. And Benjy peeked out from under the desk, apparently interested in this new activity.

Okay, Emily thought, time to focus on the Christmas presents discussion. Not a particularly happy topic for her, since she and Noelle had never received toys for Christmas.

Aunt Myra always got them something that they didn't want, but that Aunt Myra thought they should want. A piece of china or linen or artwork. Something for their future home, the home they would live in when they married.

Emily closed her eyes, inhaled deeply, and let go. "We'll take turns talking about what we hope we'll get for Christmas," she said. "You can introduce yourself to our visitor and then—"

"What's his name?" Ryan asked.

"Mark," Sandra said.

"No, it's Doctor Mark." Joanne corrected her.

"Is somebody sick?" Nathan wanted to know.

"Is somebody going to die?" Lucas asked, sounding concerned.

"You can call him Mark," Emily said, quickly, hoping they would not go off on a death tangent again.

"We'll take turns," Emily repeated. "Say your name and then tell us what you hope you'll get for Christmas."

Scrunching up their eyes and looking at the ceiling or down at the mat, they gave the question a lot of thought. A minute later, in no particular order, they began.

"My name is Nathan," Nathan said. "For Christmas, I'm getting a bike. A red one."

A bike would be nice, if the family could afford it, Emily thought. "So, you're hoping Santa will bring you a bike."

"I know he will." Nathan smiled brightly. "I saw it in the garage behind my dad's four-wheeler."

"Okay." Emily nodded. "That's a reasonable assumption."

"What are you getting for Christmas, Miss Emily?" Leslie wanted to know.

"I have no idea."

"What do you want?" Jillian asked.

"She'd like a table," Mark said.

"To eat on?" Leslie and Jillian said together.

"Yes," Mark told them.

"You don't have a table?" Jillian sounded fascinated by the idea.

"I don't need a table. I eat at the counter. Usually. Okay, Francine. It's your turn." Maybe once Francine told them what she was getting for Christmas, they could move on to a different activity.

"My name is Francine and I want sparkle paints."

Before she could elaborate, Bobby said, "My name is Bobby and I want a dog like that, too." He pointed to Makita. "What's its name?"

"This is Makita," Mark told them.

"Is that a boy or a girl?" Kyle asked.

"She's a girl dog."

"I don't care if I get a girl dog or a boy dog, I just want a dog. But I don't think my dad will let me have one," Kyle said.

"Me either," Ryan said.

"My mom will, but not my dad," Kyle elaborated. "My mom might have to sneak a dog under the Christmas tree."

"No," Ryan told Kyle. "That won't work. Your dad will figure it out."

"Okay," Emily said, stopping the discussion. "If you want a dog, your parents probably should also want a dog."

"You could get a goldfish," Brian said. "Your dad could stand a goldfish."

Emily held up her hand, the room settled and all was quiet again.

"Who's next?" she asked.

No one answered as they thought carefully about the possibilities, and again Emily had her doubts about this exercise. The last thing she wanted was for them to wish for something and then be disappointed on Christmas morning. As she was about to change the subject, she heard a tiny voice, a voice just above a whisper.

"My name is Benjy." Benjy poked his head out from under the desk, like a turtle peeking out of his shell.

This was the first time since she'd been here that Benjy had volunteered anything. The children must have sensed that too. They waited, quietly, for Benjy to say more.

"I want a new mother and father," he said.

A thick beat of silence fell over the room, and then Mark asked, "What's wrong with your old mother and father?"

Benjy moved a little further out from under the desk. "They died," he said, with his small voice.

The silence stayed and a hard band clamped around Emily's heart. It took her a moment to find her voice. "I didn't know."

"Their car crashed," Keith told her.

"Was there a lot of blood?" Nathan asked.

"I'm not allowed to watch blood on TV," Lucas added.

"I'm sorry, Benjy," Emily said, hoping her voice wouldn't shake.

"I'm sorry too," Mark said.

The questions and comments stopped.

Benjy crawled a little further out from under the desk and reached his hand to Makita. The dog licked the little boy's hand.

"That's okay," Mark said. "You can pet her."

And then, wonder of wonders, Benjy crawled all the way out, and climbed into Mark's lap. Makita put her head on Benjy's knee and the child put his arms around the dog.

At that exact moment, the classroom door swung open and Mrs. Mistle charged into the room. "Did he say he uses that dog for driving?"

Chapter Sixteen

A thrill of hope

When Mrs. Mistle saw Benjy with Makita, she spun on her heel and left the classroom. The children gave up talking about Christmas presents and gathered round Mark and Makita and Benjy. They took turns petting Makita, who was completely at ease with all of them. Benjy stayed on Mark's lap, and there was no further talk of death.

How had she missed this?

Thinking back, everyone must have assumed Mrs. Mistle had told her, and Mrs. Mistle must have assumed someone else had told her. It was a wonder the child was at school. Then again, maybe getting back into a regular routine was for the best.

And the grandmother? She would be coping in her own way—making roast beef sandwiches for Benjy, when she was probably making them for the child she had lost.

Emily's heart ached when she thought about it. What a sad Christmas for Benjy and his family—for what was left of his family.

Finally the school buzzer-like bell sounded. The children got dressed in their outdoor things. Benjy went to his cubby on his own and got dressed by himself. Keith and Brian stood near him, but Benjy seemed a little more confident. He gave Makita one last hug and left for the bus.

And then Emily was alone with Mark. He still sat on the teacher's chair beside the big teacher's desk.

On the other side of the room, she stood on the checkerboard mat, wondering what to say to him.

Suddenly, Noelle burst into the classroom.

"Em? Do you want a ride—" And then she saw Mark and quickly added, "because I can't take you today. Mark, can you give her a ride home?" Without waiting for an answer, Noelle disappeared.

"I can get home fine," Emily said.

"I'll drive you."

"You don't—"

"I'm sorry about that . . . about Benjy," Mark said. "I know it was hard for you."

"It wasn't."

He stood, walked to the edge of the checkerboard mat. "It was," he said. "Your parents died when you weren't much older than Benjy."

Mark moved even closer, until he stood right in front of her.

She felt herself shaking, and she tried to breathe deeply. *I know I'm breathing in. I know I'm breathing out.* And then Mark put his arms around her, pulled her close, and she started to cry.

She tried to push away from him, but he wouldn't let her. And she tried to stop crying but she couldn't, which was strange, because she had never been the one who cried. Only Noelle had cried, and Noelle had cried for months after the accident. Emily had been the strong one and Aunt Myra had commended her for that.

But now she was crying for Benjy, and she knew she was crying for herself too. It was as if a fragile dam had broken apart and the years of keeping the feeling controlled were gushing out.

She kept on crying, alternating between loud sobbing

and soft whimpering as her body continued to shake. It could have been five minutes, it could have been ten, it could have been more. And all the while, Mark held her firmly in his arms. Her constant Mark. She wanted nothing more than to stay in his arms forever.

Finally, as the sorrow subsided, Emily heard the door open, and then quietly close again.

Pulling away, she said, "I think I'd better—"

"Don't worry. He's gone."

"Who was there?"

"Some guy in a Santa hat."

Mr. Valentine. Whatever he wanted, she'd find out tomorrow. She was too tired to talk to anyone now. Besides, she wasn't sure if she would start crying again. For the moment though, she felt better. Lighter, somehow.

"Come on," Mark said. He helped her into her coat and led her out of the classroom and down the empty hallway, with Makita following beside them. Then he drove her home, all the while leaving her to her thoughts.

Her long ago thoughts of that long ago time when her world had collapsed and all she'd wanted to do was hide. Except she couldn't hide. She'd needed to be there for her sister. She'd needed to be strong for her sister.

The SUV stopped, and Emily noticed that Mark had not parked. Rather, he'd pulled up to the entrance of Winward Groves.

"Do you want me to come up?"

"No." She'd spoken quickly. She knew she needed to talk to him about what had happened the last time he'd been here, but she couldn't do it tonight.

"I didn't think so," he said. "You get some rest. We'll talk later. I promise." He came around, opened her door and walked with her to the entrance. Then he hugged her and kissed her forehead. "Go."

She felt him watching her as she waited for the elevator but she didn't turn around.

An hour later, after a long hot bath and a cool glass of Chardonnay, Emily dressed in her pajamas and her warm socks and, even though she knew what she'd find, she checked the fridge. As she studied the empty shelves, there was a tap on the apartment door.

Dan?

Seriously?

Would he ever give up?

But no, it was a light tap-tap-tapping, and a cheerful female voice calling her name. "Emily? Emily? Are you there?"

Mrs. Harcourt? How had Mrs. Harcourt known she would be staring at her empty fridge?

A quick check of the peep hole confirmed it really was Mrs. Harcourt, and she was holding a square box. Emily opened the door.

"Oh? Were you sleeping, dear?" Mrs. Harcourt asked as she looked at Emily's pajamas.

"No," Emily said, "I was just getting ready for bed." She stared at the box, a cardboard box with green and red stripes. "Is that pizza? Did you order pizza?" Mrs. Harcourt was definitely holding a pizza box, and the aroma was overwhelmingly delicious.

"No, not me," Mrs. Harcourt answered. "That nice young man. The one you introduced me to last week."

Last week? Did she mean . . . "Mark?"

"Yes, Mark. He was just here."

"He was?"

"He must have known you wouldn't answer your buzzer, so he buzzed me," Mrs. Harcourt said, placing the box in Emily's hands.

"Thank you," Emily said, not sure what to think. "I feel like I should be giving you some roses for this."

"No." Mrs. Harcourt beamed. "Not roses. Mark gave me the most beautiful bouquet of daisies."

"Daisies?" Emily thought about that and wondered if she might have fallen asleep and this was a dream.

"Yes, daisies," Mrs. Harcourt said, smiling, as she walked back to her apartment. "I think he's a keeper."

The next day, the Christmas concert went off without a hitch.

Mr. Valentine and Mrs. Mistle organized the ECS students who sang Jingle Bells with hand motions to mimic jingling the bells.

Emily sat with Benjy in the audience. The little boy snuggled close to his grandmother and the two of them even smiled a few times during the performance.

And then school was over for the holidays. The teachers, students, parents and other visitors left with a flurry of winter clothes and goodbyes.

When the dust settled, the floor of the main hallway held a few lost mittens, some stray pieces of wrapping paper, a broken strand of red beads, an artificial poinsettia with a twisted stem, and some green sparkles.

All ready for the janitor to sweep away.

On the following day, the twenty-third, Emily and Noelle decided to hide out from Aunt Myra by going to the Zoo.

"I'm supposed to get married tomorrow," Noelle said. "Aunt Myra will be obsessing over everything that she hasn't been able to control, and I am going to relax."

"It's a perfect plan," Emily told her sister as they sat

on the train and watched the cold gray world flash by. Neither of them had felt like driving, even though the roads were clear of ice and snow—thanks to the recent Chinooks.

The mid-morning train was mostly empty. Near the front of the car, two older ladies chattered about turkey stuffing. Across the aisle a young girl studied her cell phone and rapidly skimmed over its surface with her index finger. The last-minute shoppers were already shopping. The people who had to work were at work.

"She's still complaining about my dress," Noelle said.

Naturally Aunt Myra was still complaining. She didn't like the simple dress Noelle had chosen. But Emily did.

Noelle's floor-length dress was white with capped lace sleeves and a bodice of delicate clear Swarovski crystals. A silver band trimmed the empire waistline and soft chiffon cascaded beneath it. In that dress, her sister looked carefree and happy.

"She bought me a veil," Noelle said. "In case I change my mind at the last minute."

Emily sighed. "Please don't change your mind."

Instead of a veil, Noelle would wear a band of flowers that circled her head, and she would wear her hair long, although Aunt Myra would have preferred an elaborate swept-up style.

As the maid of honor, Emily had chosen a blue chiffon dress with a natural waistline. It was floor-length, sleeveless, and it had a jeweled neckline made of dark blue Swarovski crystals. According to Noelle, the crystals brought out the blue of Emily's eyes.

"She also bought me a cloak," Noelle said, staring out the window as the train careened along.

Oh no. That meant Aunt Myra was still hoping to transport Noelle from their Valley Ridge home to the Country Club.

"It's pretty," Noelle said. "White silk, almost floor-length, faux fur trimmed, and it has a hood."

"She's hoping you'll change your mind at the last possible instant and have to travel to the Country Club."

"I know." Noelle was quiet for a few moments. "But it is pretty. It's soft and warm and it would have worked if I'd been going anywhere cold."

The automated voice on the train announced the Zoo. Emily and Noelle de-boarded and found the ticket booth. A few minutes later, they arrived on the grounds.

Lights were strung everywhere—around branches and tree trunks and in elaborate displays depicting animals and flowers and hearts. After sunset, the Zoo would re-open for ZooLights and the landscape would be transformed into a Winter Wonderland.

For now, everything was a dreary gray. If there had been snow, it would have looked brighter, but there was no snow, and none in the forecast.

"Poor Aunt Myra," Noelle said. "No Country Club wedding and no white Christmas wedding either."

"Let's not think about Aunt Myra today." Because, Emily knew, Aunt Myra would never be satisfied, no matter what.

"Agreed," Noelle answered.

"Don't you wish you could be in Las Vegas right now?" Emily asked. Once again, her mind went to that happy time, a short two and a half weeks ago, when she and Mark had been married.

Noelle stumbled on an uneven part of the path. "What did you say?"

For the tiniest second, Emily wondered if she'd spoken aloud.

No, of course, she hadn't. "I said, don't you wish you could be in Las Vegas? Right now? It was so warm there for your Jack and Jill party."

"Yes." Noelle coughed. "Yes, it was."

She sounded like she might be coming down with a cold. Emily hoped not, because the last thing this wedding needed was for the bride to get sick.

"I enjoyed that trip." Noelle's voice sounded even again, and somehow, wistful. "I enjoyed it a lot."

"I like winter too." And Emily did. She liked the cold crispness of the season. "Let's get some hot chocolate and stand by one of the fires."

As they headed toward the concession to buy hot chocolate, Noelle's cell phone rang and they paused on the sidewalk.

"Better not answer that," Emily said, worried it could be Aunt Myra.

"It might be Troy," Noelle said as she checked the display, and then, "Oh!" and she answered. "Hello?" A pause while she listened. "Yes, right now. We're at the Zoo. Don't tell Aunt Myra."

The caller, probably Troy, spoke for a minute or so, and Noelle nodded at the words. "Okay, I suppose." And then, "No. It will be fine. Five minutes." She ended the call.

"Who was that?"

"Mark." Noelle looked puzzled.

"Mark?" *Calling Noelle?* "What did he want?"

"Actually, he was calling you, but you have your phone turned off."

Right. She did.

"He needs to talk to you in person."

"He does?"

"I think he wants to surprise me with something tomorrow."

"Really?"

"He said he only needs five minutes and then he promises he'll disappear. Because today is for you and me."

"He's coming to the Zoo?"

"Yes." Noelle shrugged, as they walked to the little

concession. "He's meeting us at noon. At the cafeteria."

"And he can't talk to me on the phone?"

"He says it has to be in person."

"Okay." It was probably something to do with the chapel and finding the missing paperwork.

"Hot chocolate and fire pit first," Noelle said. "Then we'll go to the Conservatory. I want to see tropical plants, and the butterflies."

Mark sat with Pro in the ER staffroom at the Nose Hill Hospital. He'd just told Pro what he'd learned about Las Vegas. Pro was quiet, apparently thinking about the options.

Mark looked out the window at the barren patio with its old wrought iron bench and the low evergreen shrubs. Leftover autumn leaves and bits of twigs lay strewn across the patio stones and all traces of the snowman were gone.

Kit Livingston poked his head into the room. "The chopper is five minutes out."

"I'll be right there," Mark said, then took one last sip of his coffee. He looked at Pro.

"Interesting."

"I know. Now what?"

"Depends," Pro said. "What do you want to do?"

Mark grinned. "Since we can't get a marriage certificate from the Clark County Recorder's Office, we'll go to the Registry in Crowfoot. It will be open tomorrow, at least until noon."

"You mean . . . a marriage *license*," Pro said.

"Yes."

Pro stared at him. "You're sure?"

"Yes. I am."

"You'll need to take Emily with you."

"I know."

"What are you going to tell her?"

Mark shrugged. "That we need the marriage certificate?"

Pro considered a moment. "Seems reasonable," he said.

"She'll be distracted with last minute stuff for Noelle. And with keeping her aunt happy."

"And?" Pro added, "she knows you need the document."

Mark glanced at the clock on the wall above the coffee pot. "I'll deal with this skiing accident and then I need to get to the Zoo."

At noon, Emily and Noelle headed for the Kitamba Café.

"There's Mark," Noelle said. "You get five minutes."

"I know."

"I'll pick up some soup. And sandwiches. And coffee. We can eat outside by the penguin enclosure." Noelle breezed up to Mark. They greeted each other by slapping palms together, and then Noelle disappeared inside the building.

Emily waited, her heart suddenly pounding, as Mark approached.

He put his arm around her. "Come over here," he said as he guided her toward the nearby fire pit.

They sat on one of the benches that surrounded the fire. No one else was there. Mark took his arm away and turned to face her. "Here's the thing," he said, and he paused, as if searching for words. It was so unlike him, to not be able to say what he wanted.

The awkward silence made her stomach churn. "You kissed me," she blurted.

He tilted his head, studying her a moment. "Yes, I did."

A tiny pause. "And you kissed me."

"I—I mean—"

"Would you like to kiss me again?"

She closed her eyes, and wished he could be serious, just for once. "I—Judith—"

"Don't worry about it." His eyes twinkled, her forever lighthearted Mark.

"But—"

"It wasn't serious with Judith."

"It's never serious with—" Wait a minute. "What do you mean . . . *wasn't?*"

"We were never serious and we aren't seeing each other anymore." He spoke simply, as if they were discussing the lack of snow in the forecast. Then he asked, "What happened that night?"

That night? In her apartment? "When we kissed?"

"No, when you left your rehearsal dinner?"

"Oh. That." Where was this conversation going? "Nothing much," she said. Only that she'd come to her senses at the last minute.

"Something must have happened." He waited, watching her eyes.

She'd never wanted to talk about that night because she'd felt so incredibly stupid to have let things go so far. But, what did it matter now. "Easy," she said, with a shrug. "I figured out I wasn't in love with Dan."

Mark smiled. "Good." And then, "I found the chapel in Las Vegas."

What? No other questions about that night? And just as quickly, he'd forgotten about their kiss. Apparently they were back to being friends.

"Okay, you found the chapel. That's good," she said. But it didn't feel good. It meant that they would no longer be married—not that they were really married anyway.

"Yes," he continued. "The regular officiant was off that night, so there was a replacement."

"A replacement?"

"And the paperwork wasn't done correctly, so we have to go to the Registry tomorrow."

"Tomorrow? I can't. I've got to help Noelle tomorrow. Aunt Myra will be—"

"It won't take long."

Emily sighed. Maybe it would be best to do it tomorrow. To get it over with before the holidays.

"I'll pick you up about noon and take you to the Registry in Crowfoot."

"To get the marriage certificate?" Or whatever documents they needed to get the marriage certificate sent from Las Vegas.

"The marriage license, at this point," he said.

And hopefully Aunt Myra would not be driving Noelle crazy. The paperwork was probably sitting in Las Vegas and the Registry needed to send them something to speed things up. "And I need to be there?"

"Yes. Bring your driver's license and your passport. It should only take a few minutes. Not many people will be picking up licenses tomorrow."

"Okay. But then I have to help Noelle."

"I'll have you back to your apartment in lots of time to get ready for the wedding."

"No," she said. "You should take me right to Aunt Myra's. I'll bring my clothes. I can get ready with Noelle and I won't have to worry about finding a bus to Valley Ridge."

"Ryder will be driving past Winward Groves on his way to Myra's house," Mark told her, sounding confident about the details. "He'll pick you up about four."

"Four o'clock? But—"

"There's Noelle. I'd better go. I know she wants to

spend today with you." He kissed her forehead, a light quick touch. "I'll see you at noon tomorrow." And before Emily could ask another question, he was gone.

Noelle arrived, holding a cafeteria tray laden with sandwiches, steaming bowls of soup and hot coffee. "That was fast," she said. She sat on the bench and placed the tray between them.

"Um, yes. He said Ryder will pick me up tomorrow at four o'clock."

"That works," Noelle said.

"But don't you want me there earlier?"

"No need. My mind will be up in the air but I've got everything ready to go."

"Are you sure? I can be there to help you . . ."

"If he picks you up at four, you'll be at Aunt Myra's in twenty minutes. Ceremony is at half past five. That's plenty of time."

"But won't Aunt Myra be—"

"Don't worry about Aunt Myra. I told her I want to be alone in my room to get ready and she seems all right with that."

And so did Noelle seem all right about that. In fact, Noelle seemed too calm.

"So, is Mark going to surprise me with something tomorrow?"

Right. The surprise. "Then it wouldn't be a surprise," Emily said. Besides, as far as she knew, there was no surprise. Mark had simply wanted to tell her he'd found the chapel and for some reason they were picking up extra paperwork tomorrow.

"It's okay," Noelle said. "Do you want to eat over by the penguin enclosure?" She glanced that way. "Oh! Look! The penguins are out!"

And so, with Noelle carrying their loaded cafeteria tray, they meandered up the path and found a place to sit. Then they watched the penguins, all dressed up in their tuxedo best and strutting along two by two.

Chapter Seventeen

We wish you a Merry Christmas!

It was December twenty-fourth and, finally, this Christmas Eve wedding would happen. Not quite the way it had been planned, but it would happen.

Catherine Forsythe parked outside Myra's Valley Ridge estate home. The Christmas lights twinkled, the air was frosty, and if the fates approved, there might even be snow later in the evening. It would be so wonderful if Myra could have her white Christmas wedding. But, at the very least, she would have her Country Club wedding.

The details were all taken care of. The Swan Room looked beautiful. The officiant had been notified and the guests had been notified. Everyone knew about the change in venue, except for Noelle and Troy. And, of course, Emily.

Myra had simply decided to stop arguing. At five o'clock, she would tell Noelle that everyone was at the Country Club. No one had told Emily because she would have told Noelle, and there would have been a scene. As it was, Noelle would not make a scene. She would go along with her aunt's wishes, like she always did.

Emily was such a bad influence.

Still sitting in her car, Catherine checked the time. A quarter past four. The ceremony would take place at five-thirty. Hopefully, Myra was not having any problems with Noelle. But, if there were problems, that's why Catherine was here. To smooth things over.

The guests were beginning to arrive at the Country Club. Logan's girlfriend, Cheryl, was already there. Logan should have been with her, but he'd decided to meet his friends here.

For some reason Logan and Ryder and Pro and Mark all wanted to go to the wedding together. It didn't make any sense but it was some weird logic they had. Something about all being on the same football team in high school.

Men. They could be so troublesome.

Of course, they knew about the change of venue. They didn't think it was a particularly good idea but it wasn't for them to decide. At least, they had agreed not to say anything to Emily.

Besides the venue change, Myra had made another executive decision: Dan would be the best man. Troy's original choice—Jeff—hadn't minded at all when Myra and Catherine had told him.

He'd laughed and said, "Sure thing. Fine with me."

So he obviously didn't care about being replaced.

Dan would be picking up Troy, right about now, and taking him to the Country Club.

As Catherine was opening the car door, her cell rang. The readout said *Dan*. Now what? She closed the door again. "Hello?"

"Catherine?"

"Yes?"

"It's Troy. I mean, it's Dan," Dan said. "Troy's not here."

"What do you mean, *he's not here?*"

"He's not at his apartment. Is he at Noelle's house?"

Catherine pressed her thumb and index finger to the

space between her brows. *Stupid, stupid.* Why would Troy leave early? And why couldn't Dan keep track of the groom. That was his job!

"You can't find Troy?"

"That's what I'm telling you. Are you at Noelle's house?"

"I got here a minute ago."

"And?"

"I haven't gone inside yet." She saw Ryder's truck pulling up.

"If he's at Noelle's house," Dan said, "should I come over?"

Catherine watched as Ryder got out of his truck. He wore a black tux and, she had to admit, he looked impressive. But for *their* wedding, he'd be wearing gray because gray was one of her colors. She didn't care if he didn't like gray.

"Catherine?" Dan's voice came from the phone.

"Let me think." She watched as Ryder walked around to the passenger side and opened the door for someone. A woman dressed in a red coat. *Emily?*

How come she wasn't here already? She should have been here by now to help her sister. Honestly, some people had no sense of priorities.

No doubt, Emily had had issues with getting a ride. She should have borrowed Myra's car yesterday but do you think she would have thought that far ahead? No.

She wore her hair up, the soft blonde waves rising to the back of her head. It looked simple and elegant at the same time.

As Ryder and Emily came around the truck, Catherine saw Emily's blue gown blowing in the breeze. Besides the red coat and the blue gown, she wore her white rabbit fur Mukluks. She was carrying her shoes—silver, strappy sandals—looped around her mitts. She was also carrying a box. A plain box, not gift wrapped. Had she brought extra shoes?

"Catherine?" Dan asked, again.

Catherine heaved out a breath. "Go to the Country Club and wait there. I'll find Troy."

If Ryder and Logan and Pro and Mark were leaving together from Myra's, Troy was probably here with them.

Emily had a feeling it would snow tonight. Somehow, there would be big fluffy snowflakes in time for the wedding. In a little over an hour, her sister would be married in front of the fireplace in their childhood home.

With Ryder beside her, Emily hurried up the sidewalk, carrying her dress shoes and Aunt Myra's carefully wrapped unicorn. She could hardly wait to see her sister.

"Ryder!"

They both turned and saw Catherine walking toward them. Her hair was styled with cascading ringlets. Her long earrings glittered and her black fur-trimmed cloak fluttered in the slight breeze.

When she reached them, she said, "I didn't know you were bringing Emily."

"Mark organized that," Ryder said. "He was worried about being late, coming from the hospital."

"But he will be here?"

"I think he's here now. That's his SUV. Over there." Ryder pointed to Frank's driveway.

Mark was either inside, or still at his dad's house. If he was at his dad's, Emily hoped he'd be here soon. Because she needed him for moral support in case Aunt Myra tried to meddle at the last moment.

It was all Emily could think about. How Aunt Myra could sabotage Noelle's wedding day. But, surprisingly, Noelle was calm. At least, she was yesterday, as they'd walked around the Zoo. It was as if she was entirely confident that everything would happen perfectly.

Earlier today, Mark and Emily had dashed into the Registry at Crowfoot. Taking her passport, he'd filled out the forms while she paced.

"What if Aunt Myra sends everyone to the Country Club?" Emily lamented.

"Don't worry about it," Mark said. "What's your mother's maiden name?"

Emily spelled it for him. "And who knows what she's told the officiant!"

"The officiant will be at the house," Mark said as he wrote on the form. "Ryder has talked to him. What's your father's middle name?"

Emily told him and continued to pace. The clerk seemed to be looking at her with an odd expression.

Mark asked her a few more questions, like where her parents had been born, and then he handed her a pen. "Sign here," he said, and she did. And then he handed the forms to the clerk. A few minutes later, Mark had a piece of paper in his hands and they were leaving.

He continued to reassure her, telling her everything would be fine, no matter what Aunt Myra might have engineered. And then he had returned her to her apartment by a quarter to one.

When she'd stepped off the elevator, Mrs. Harcourt was there, with a kale and cranberry salad. "A little something for your special day," Mrs. Harcourt had said. Well, she meant Noelle's special day, but who cared. The salad made a delicious lunch.

After lunch, Emily did some yoga and had a nice long bath. Then she dressed carefully in the blue gown that she and Noelle had picked out. When Ryder buzzed her unit at four o'clock, she was ready to go. On the way to Valley Ridge, Ryder told her everything was taken care of and there was no need to worry about anything.

Still, until it was over, something could go wrong.

Now they stood on the doorstep in the cool air and Emily thought she felt a snowflake on her cheek.

"Do you really have to drive over with them?" Catherine asked.

"Yes," Ryder answered. "It's part of the contract I signed for being their friend."

"You're impossible." Catherine laughed. "Let's go inside."

As they walked into the house, the bells on the door jingled, and Aunt Myra came rushing over to meet them. "I'm so glad you're here!" She wore her purple dress with the frills, overdone makeup and a purple feather in her hair.

Catherine frowned. "Is something wrong?"

"No, but that man is driving me crazy!" Aunt Myra vibrated as she spoke, and the feather bounced.

"Who?"

"Prometheus Jones. He's been here since—" Aunt Myra checked her watch. "Since one-thirty!"

"And?" Catherine prompted.

Emily's brows came together. Maybe Pro wanted to be helpful? Although one-thirty was a bit early. Even for Pro.

"He's been drinking cinnamon tea and eating cookies and asking me so . . . many . . . questions!"

Normally, Aunt Myra loved answering questions and giving her opinions but, apparently, even she had a limit.

"And then Logan Nicholas showed up at two-thirty. He's just as bad."

"Is Noelle downstairs?" Emily asked, slipping out of her Mukluks.

"Of course she is!" Aunt Myra turned to her. "And you!" she said. "*You* should have been here earlier!"

"But Noelle didn't want—"

"I don't care what Noelle wants. You're her sister. And

you're her maid of honor. The two of you should be getting ready together. All this nonsense about *needing some space*." Aunt Myra inclined her head toward the hallway and the back of the house. "Even those two," she said. "Every time I say I should check on Noelle, they tell me it's *not a good idea to disturb the bride*," she mimicked. "As if they would know anything about it. And now they're talking about helicopter rides over the city."

Catherine cleared her throat. "Myra, let me introduce my fiancé."

"Of course." Aunt Myra collected herself, and her feather settled.

"This is Ryder O'Callaghan," Catherine said. "And, this is Emily's aunt, Myra."

They shook hands.

"Pardon me," Aunt Myra said. "I'm simply overwhelmed with all this planning."

"I'm sure you can relax," Ryder said, as he took Emily's coat and hung it in the closet. "Everything will happen the way it's supposed to."

"I'm glad someone thinks so." Aunt Myra turned to Emily again. "Now, Emily, you'd better check on Noelle. She won't mind if *you* go down."

If only Aunt Myra could let the day happen without getting upset about something. Emily wondered if she should go downstairs right away, or take the time to put on her sandals.

"What's in that box?" Aunt Myra asked.

Emily dropped her shoes on the floor. "Your unicorn."

"Oh! The unicorn! It's about time you brought it back. Now Noelle can have it after the ceremony."

Ryder smiled. "A unicorn has something to do with the ceremony?"

Emily glanced up at him. "Don't ask."

"Bring it over here," Aunt Myra said.

And just that quickly, it was no longer important that Emily rush downstairs to check on her sister. Her sister could wait until the unicorn had been given its due respect.

Aunt Myra led the way to the kitchen, and Emily followed, feeling the cold tile on her feet.

A teapot, three teacups and a half-empty tray of Aunt Myra's Christmas cookies ranged across the dining room table. Pro and Logan sat at either end. Like Ryder, they wore black tuxedos.

Emily entered the kitchen and set her box on the granite counter that divided the kitchen and dining room. Aunt Myra stood on her left. Ryder stood on her right. Pro and Logan got up from the table and came over to see what was going on.

Meanwhile, Catherine walked to the Christmas tree in the living room and studied the angel on top of the tree. "Where's Troy?"

Probably downstairs with Noelle, Emily thought, as she took the lid off the box. From behind her, she heard the bells on the door jingle again.

"That must be Frank," Aunt Myra said, still waiting to see her unicorn.

Emily pulled back a sheet of tissue paper, and hoped that Mark was with his dad.

"Any time today!" Aunt Myra nudged her. "Could you please hurry up?"

Frank arrived in the kitchen, also wearing a black tux. Looking at the other men, he said, "My! Don't we look dapper!"

No sign of Mark. Emily wondered where he was and, again, hoped he'd be here soon. She scrunched away the rest of the tissue paper, and exposed the unicorn.

"Perfect. Simply perfect." Aunt Myra sighed. "Just what Noelle needs."

Light danced off the glittering crystal as Emily rotated

it. But, never mind the way it caught the light, something about the unicorn seemed malevolent.

Sitting beside Frank, Makita woofed. A large red bow had been attached to the back of the dog's collar.

Catherine joined them at the counter. "Is Troy—" She stopped, and stared at Makita.

"There is no way you are bringing that dog to the Country Club!"

Frank cocked his head, knit his brows. "The Country Club? Why would I bring her to the Country Club?"

Emily gripped the unicorn and a chill ran down her spine. "The Country Club?"

"Now, Emily, there wasn't enough room for all the guests here," Aunt Myra said.

She didn't. She couldn't. How could Aunt Myra do this? The hard, jagged crystal . . . the spike of the horn, the flare of the tail poked against the soft pads of Emily's hands.

"But, Noelle wants to be married here, in a simple ceremony, in front of the fireplace."

Across from her, with elbows leaning on the granite counter, Logan said, "Much better to get married in the sky."

"The sky?" Catherine squinted. "What are you talking about?"

"In a helicopter." Pro laughed.

"Have they been drinking?" Catherine asked Aunt Myra. "And where is Troy?"

But Aunt Myra wasn't listening. She narrowed her eyes, as she looked out at the backyard. "What is he doing?"

Emily glanced out the window and saw Mark. Instant relief swept over her, from the top of her head to the tips of her cold toes.

He was in the backyard and, like the others, he was wearing a black tux. He looked so tall and handsome and . . . so forever out of reach to her.

"Oh for heaven's sake! Why is he building a fire?" Aunt Myra blustered. "We'll just have to put it out." She checked her watch. "We have to leave soon." Heading for the hallway and the stairs, she mumbled, "I should have got rid of that fire pit a long time ago." Over her shoulder, she shouted, "Emily! Tell him to put that fire out! Right now! I'm getting Noelle."

They heard Aunt Myra clomp down the stairs.

"It's what she wants, Emily," Catherine said, sitting on one of the dining room chairs.

What about what Noelle wants? Emily wished she could say the words out loud but she knew it was pointless.

"Is anyone listening to me?" Catherine looked around again. "Where is Troy?"

In the backyard, Mark leaned over the fire pit, as if he were coaxing a flame to life. Wearing her pretty red bow, Makita sat at the window watching him. Emily still held the unicorn, cradling it in both hands.

Pro and Logan stood opposite her on the other side of the granite counter. Frank was on her left. Ryder was on her right. She was surrounded by men in black tuxedos.

"Brace yourself," Ryder said.

"Pardon?"

Just then they heard a long shrill "*noooooooo . . .*" come from the basement. And then, "No! No! No! No! No!" as footsteps pounded on the stairs.

Three seconds later, Emily swung around as Aunt Myra charged into the kitchen waving a piece of paper.

"Noelle isn't here!"

"What?" Catherine stood up.

"She's eloped!" Aunt Myra shrieked, waving the piece of paper and zeroing her gaze on Emily. "This is your fault!"

My fault?

Emily stared at her aunt, studying the woman who,

right at this moment, looked comical—as she waved that piece of paper like a flag at a car race. Aunt Myra jumped up and down, and the frills of her purple dress jumped and jiggled. Then the purple feather in her hair dislodged, and slowly tipped over.

And then . . . Emily felt a sudden, strange sense of calm, as if she wasn't really here, as if she were watching this all on a screen. Holding the unicorn, she stepped away from the granite counter and further into the kitchen.

"No," she said. "It's not my fault."

And then she held the unicorn out in front of her, waited a second, and let go—watching as the crystal fell to the tile floor in slow motion, and exploded in a thousand tiny pieces.

Even after Frank had swept away the crystal splinters, Aunt Myra was still pacing in the kitchen and brandishing Noelle's letter.

"But why would she want to elope? I don't understand it!"

Pro and Logan exchanged a glance.

"Please, Myra," Catherine said, again. "Will you read the letter?"

"Oh all right!" Aunt Myra came to a stop and squared her shoulders.

"Dear Aunt Myra—

By the time you read this, we will be up in the air and on our way to get married."

Aunt Myra whipped the letter down. "I can't understand it!" she repeated. Then she stared at Emily. "And my unicorn! You did that deliberately!"

"Keep reading," Catherine said.

Myra resumed.

> *"Thanks for everything. Enjoy the party at the Country Club. Dance with Frank."*

A short pause. "Dance with Frank? Oh, honestly!"

"What else?" Catherine prodded her.

Gripping the letter, Aunt Myra read on.

> *"And please give that pretty cloak to Emily. It will look beautiful with her dress.*
>
> *Love, Noelle and Troy"*

Aunt Myra crumpled the letter with her fists. "And that is all!" She squeezed her lips into a straight line, inhaled and seemed to regain her composure. "Catherine and I will go ahead and make the announcement. Emily, you wear Noelle's cloak to the Country Club. It will look nice with that dress." And then she added, "Though why you chose blue is beyond me."

"We're still having the reception?" Frank asked.

"Of course we're still having the reception!" Aunt Myra set Noelle's letter on the counter in the kitchen. "I'm not sending everyone home simply because the bride and groom have decided not to show up."

Frank checked his watch. "Moonrise at five-thirty."

"What are you talking about?"

"Let's watch the moon rise before we go," Frank said. "It's not often you get a full moon on Christmas Eve."

Makita woofed in agreement.

"How can you think about the moon at a time like this?" Aunt Myra pressed her hands on either side of Noelle's letter, smoothing out the edges of the paper, as if that could help her make better sense of what had happened. "She must have slipped out while we were drinking tea," Aunt Myra said, thinking out loud. "But how did she get a cab here?"

How indeed, Emily thought, as she looked at Pro, and

then at Logan. They were picking up their teacups, turning them over and reading the bottoms.

"I can hardly believe it. First Emily, and now this. Where did I go wrong?"

"Myra, calm down." Catherine took charge. "You'll have your celebration. We'll drink toasts to the bride and groom. It will be a wonderful evening." She nudged Aunt Myra toward the front door. "Are you sure you don't want to come with me, Ryder?"

"We'll catch up," he said.

Aunt Myra shouted last minute instructions to Emily. Catherine and Aunt Myra donned coats. Aunt Myra's feather was repositioned. And then the house was silent, and no one stirred. Not even Makita.

Frank was the first to speak. "Good job with the unicorn," he said.

"Thanks," Emily answered, still somewhat surprised by her courage. "It felt right." She looked at Pro. "Did you drive them to the airport?"

"No, it was me," Logan said, grinning. "Pro distracted Myra while Troy and I got Noelle out the patio doors."

"Their flight has left?"

"At four o'clock."

The time on the microwave said five minutes past five. "And yesterday? At the Zoo? Noelle knew about this?"

"She has for some time," Pro said.

Good for Noelle. For taking charge of her wedding. And her life.

"Noelle didn't want to tell you," Pro continued, "because she didn't want you to have to worry about pretending you didn't know anything."

"Yes, easier this way." Besides, without any distractions, Emily and her sister had completely enjoyed their day together at the Zoo. "Where are they flying to?"

"Back to Las Vegas," Pro said. "They'll get the marriage license tonight. And they'll be married tomorrow morning, in a helicopter above the city."

"In a helicopter! And on Christmas morning!" Emily couldn't help smiling.

"You knew about their helicopter ride? Earlier this month?" Pro asked.

"Yes, I knew. And Noelle doesn't feel bad about her original plans?"

"No," Pro said. "They both want another helicopter ride over the city. They said it will be the best Christmas ever."

"And the best Christmas Eve ever," Frank said.

Mark's father was definitely in a good mood. He seemed to have enjoyed the smashing of the unicorn as much as Emily had.

They were all gathered around the granite counter, except for Mark, who was still in the backyard building up the fire.

Frank crossed the kitchen, opened the pantry door and took out a large box. A florist's box. He brought it to the counter. "This is Noelle's bouquet."

Emily lifted the top from the box, glanced at the arrangement of evergreens that she and Noelle had chosen. "I wonder what I should do with this? Put it in water for when she returns?"

"We have an idea," Ryder said, from behind her. "But first—"

He wrapped something around her shoulders. Emily felt the faux fur as it brushed her chin. Noelle's white silk cloak.

"Get your boots on and go help Mark build that fire."

· · · · ·

Looking out the patio doors, Emily took a moment to watch Mark. He stood in front of their fire pit, warming his hands, looking so handsome and dependable. She wanted to keep this image in her heart forever because she would always love him, this childhood friend of hers.

Bundled in the white cloak and wearing her warm Mukluks, she stepped outside and crossed the backyard to stand beside him. "You look good in a tux."

He turned, and when he saw her, he seemed to catch his breath. "And you look beautiful," he said. "You always do."

Then he kissed her, on her lips. She felt a shiver echo through her body and resonate in her soul. And she felt a longing for more, for something more than she could ever have.

"Umm, should we be—"

"I want to marry you."

What was he talking about? "Umm, you already did," she said. "But it didn't take."

"That's because I've been an idiot," he said. "You know how your aunt always said I would never settle down?"

"Yes, but—"

"I think she said I was commitment phobic. Something wordy like that."

"Yes, but—"

"Well, I am the most committed man you will ever know. I have loved you all these years," he said. "That's why no one else could ever find a place in my heart. You, dear Emily, have always had that place and you always will."

"I . . . I don't know what to say."

"Say you'll marry me."

"Aren't we already married?"

"No, we're not. We didn't get a marriage license the first time."

"We didn't— But Elvis had us sign something?"

"It wasn't a license. It was a chapel certificate."

"But why didn't—"

"Because he wasn't really Elvis."

She laughed. "I know he wasn't really Elvis. He's Christopher Kringle."

"Christopher Kringle was a replacement," Mark said. "The real Elvis was drunk and they had to send him home."

She remembered almost everything that had happened that night. Everything important. But the paperwork had been a blur. A confusing necessity that they had rushed through. And, right now, it was becoming more confusing. "You mean, Christopher Kringle is *not* an officiant?"

"No," Mark said. "He's a bartender. He works at the bar next door to the chapel. And he's always wanted to do a wedding."

"You mean . . . we're *not* married?"

"No, not yet." Mark wrapped both hands around hers. His were so warm, and strong, and solid.

"So . . . we don't need to get divorced?"

"No, not ever. Let's get married."

"Married? Now?"

Mark shrugged in that typically unserious way of his. "The officiant is here."

"He is?"

A quirk of a smile. "They don't need him at the Country Club."

She didn't know what to say. This could not be happening. This was a trick of the season and the wintry air and the warm fire.

"Emily? Say yes?" He got down on one knee, with the crisp black tuxedo touching the bare bricks of the patio. "Emily Marie Farrell, I've been in love with you since you took me home that day when I was in grade four. I didn't know it then. And I didn't know it when we were in Vegas, but I know it now."

Her heart stuttered. "Are you sure?"

"Perfectly. Will you marry me?"

She heard a wisp of wind in the branches of the fir trees. The scent of the burning logs filled the evening. Beside them, the fire crackled and danced. The world paused.

"Yes," she said, as a rush of joy avalanched over her and she started to laugh. "Yes. Yes. Yes."

Mark rose up and kissed her, a long full kiss. And then he took a step back and reached in his pocket.

The ring was exactly what she would have chosen. A dark blue sapphire surrounded by diamonds and set in white gold. "How did you know?"

His smile told her he was pleased. "I thought you'd like it. And," he added, "I checked with your sister."

"You've been busy."

"Yes," he said. "And after our ceremony—here, by our fire—we'll have some champagne. And then there's a limo ready to take us to Banff."

"We're going to the mountains? Tonight?"

"To the Banff Springs. I have the honeymoon suite reserved. Seems they don't have a lot of Christmas Eve weddings."

"The Banff Springs? I have to pack!"

"No, you don't. Noelle took care of the packing."

"She did? How?"

"Yesterday," he said. "She gave Mrs. Harcourt a list. Mrs. Harcourt used your emergency key."

So Mrs. Harcourt knew.

"Your suitcase is at my dad's house," Mark said. "Ready to go. Now all we need is that officiant and some witnesses."

He turned and looked at the dining room window where four men in black tuxedos stood watching.

Mark gave them a thumbs up, and they all returned it. After that, things happened very quickly.

A tall man with white hair opened the patio doors and came outside. He wore a dark suit and carried a black book and some loose papers. With him, was a young woman. She wore a beige jacket and beige pants with a down vest of the same color. And she carried a camera.

"I'm Claire," the photographer said, shaking hands with Emily. "Your sister sent me."

"Of course she did." For so long, Emily had thought she was taking care of her little sister. And now it turned out that her little sister was the one taking care of her.

"And I'm Andy Farraday, your officiant. I must say, this is a beautiful—and unique—place to get married. I love marrying people outdoors."

The photographer slipped into the background and from then on they hardly noticed her.

"Mark has given me the license," Andy said, "so we're ready to start."

"The license?"

"That's what we signed this morning at the Registry." Mark squeezed her hand. "We'll get it right this time."

So that explained it. She had seen the title of the form she was signing, but she'd been so worried about Noelle that she hadn't cared to figure out *why* they were getting a license *now*. "Yes," she said. "This time, we'll get it right."

And then Ryder came through the patio doors, carrying a bottle of champagne. Logan and Pro followed next. They brought the tall fluted glasses. The champagne and glasses were left on a makeshift table of cinder blocks and would stay chilled in the winter air.

Frank came out of the doors last, with Makita prancing beside him. Makita wore her red bow, and Frank carried Noelle's bouquet.

"For you," he said, as he handed her the mix of

evergreens and pine cones and holly berries.

Mark and Emily stood in front of the fire pit with Andy the officiant. A real officiant, this time. He opened his book and recited the magical words.

> *We are gathered here today in the presence of these friends, to join Mark and Emily in matrimony.*

In front of them, the fire burned brightly, giving off a warm glow. Ryder and Pro and Logan and Mark's father, Frank, stood in a semicircle around them. The full moon rose over the horizon.

And then the first big snowflakes started to whirl and flutter through the sky, drifting onto Mark's tuxedo and brushing Emily's eyelashes, dusting the world with whiteness . . . and promising the newlyweds a sparkling new beginning.

If you enjoyed
A WEDDING AND A WHITE CHRISTMAS
you can help others find this story
by leaving a short review at
your favorite online retailer site.

Next in the *Something Old, Something New* series is
Ryder's story—

On the Way to a Wedding

An isolated forest road, a car in the ditch, a sprained ankle,
a wedding dress . . .

Ryder O'Callaghan finds Toria Whitney on the side of a
forest road with a totaled car, a sprained ankle, and a
wedding dress. Both Ryder and Toria are scheduled to be
married in three weeks—but not to each other.

Find more books by Suzanne Stengl at
www.SuzanneStengl.com

About the Author

I've been telling stories since I was a child. Then, it was stories about fairies and mermaids, told to my sisters when we were supposed to be sleeping. As a teenager, I wrote long diary entries and I wrote short pieces of fiction—that no one but me ever read.

Don't get me wrong, I was not a total recluse. I did lots of "real world" things too. I became a nurse, I spent time with friends, I traveled a lot. And I always wrote.

Sometimes after a difficult day at work, I would re-create the day in a story that had a better ending. That's still what I do—I create stories with happy, hopeful endings.

"Suzanne Stengl has a lovely voice with a subtle hint of humor."
—*A.M. Westerling, author of A Knight for Love*

"Suzanne Stengl's descriptions and characters are really memorable."
—*Amy Jo Fleming, author of Death at Bandit Creek*

CPSIA information can be obtained
at www.ICGtesting.com
Printed in the USA
LVOW11s0914130418
573189LV00001B/2/P